THE
ASSISI MURDERS

THE
ASSISI MURDERS

Timothy Holme

Walker and Company
New York

Library of Congress Cataloging-in-Publication Data

Holme, Timothy.
  The Assisi murders / Timothy Holme.
    p. cm.
  ISBN 0-8027-5721-9
  I. Title.
PR6058.045355A78 1988   823'.914—dc19   88-12662

All the characters and events portrayed in this story are
fictitious.

Published in the United States of America in 1988
by the Walker Publishing Company, Inc.

Printed in the United States of America

10 9 8 7 6 5 4 3 2 1

Maria Grazia, with love

A Brush with the Camorra

As a policeman, Commissario Achille Peroni was accustomed to early hours, but he never enjoyed them. The idea of getting up early when you didn't have to seemed to him preposterous, and a four a.m. alarm this morning to catch a five a.m. coach for a journey he didn't want to make in the first place had left him in an extremely bad temper.

Still dark outside. Shapes of buildings and trees loomed anonymously as the coach passed them. The rest of Verona obviously agreed with Peroni about early hours, for it was still emphatically in bed, and even the traffic lights, flashing yellow at all comers, were not yet on duty.

Darkness hid the other occupants of the coach which, as far as Peroni was concerned, was just as well. He was quite convinced that the only thing he could possibly have in common with any of them was a dislike of getting out of bed early.

'You might look as though you were enjoying yourself, Achille.' Peroni's sister, Assunta. The cause of the trouble.

'I'm not enjoying myself, so why should I look as if I were?'

The coach halted while the driver took a ticket at the check-in station, then started to roll along the approach road to the autostrada.

He shouldn't have been there at all. The whole thing was the upshot of a futile and apparently pointless episode. Much against his will, Peroni had been tipped into a complicated enquiry into Camorra activities in Venice where he was stationed. The Camorra is a Neapolitan version of the Mafia, and Peroni could not conceive why he of all people – himself a Neopolitan – should have been picked on to direct this particular enquiry. 'Set a thief to catch a thief,' one colleague had suggested. Peroni had not found this funny.

The enquiry had been dragging on for months now. The basis of it was that the Camorra had been expanding its activities in the north of Italy, particularly Venice and the rest of the Veneto. This expansion was being skilfully controlled by an anonymous Camorra boss from an undiscovered headquarters. The aim of the enquiry was to identify man and place, but in all the mass of information which Peroni and two assistants had accumulated there was nothing which gave them a line onto either.

That had been the situation three days previously when Peroni – his erotic engines turning lazily over as he eyed Venetian pulchritude – rounded the corner into a quiet *calle* near San Zaccaria and literally bumped into Spaghetti.

Spaghetti had been so nicknamed because his arms and legs were so long and thin that they put you in mind of the national pasta. He was by no means in the higher councils of the Camorra; more an errand boy, but as such he knew all sorts of things, and Peroni had been wanting to speak to him for a long time.

'Spaghetti!' Peroni greeted him as an old friend which, in a sense, he was. But Spaghetti obviously wasn't in a mood for friendship. He stared for an instant, then turned and ran.

Normal underground reaction to the police was to start cajoling or bargaining, so this sudden flight took Peroni by surprise. Spaghetti, he thought as he started to pursue, must be carrying something very delicate indeed.

Those long, thin legs had surprising vigour in them, and Spaghetti was off to a good start, heading in the direction of San Marco.

Early tourists, brandishing cameras and making mental translations of lira into their own currencies, jumped out of the way with expressions which said *Italia, Italia!* as the flailing-limbed Camorra bit player panted by with the Rudolph Valentino of the Italian police in hot pursuit.

They crossed over a canal which gave them the opportunity to enjoy an admirable view of the Bridge of Sighs on their left, but neither of them took advantage of it.

The nearer they came to San Marco the denser grew the crowd, and the chase deteriorated into a succession of dodgings, leapings and spurts, but Peroni was starting to narrow the distance between them.

As they came out into Piazza San Marco, Spaghetti started cutting right towards the Mercerie, and Peroni reckoned to grab him before he entered it.

He would have done, too, if Spaghetti hadn't taken out a gun and fired it at him.

For an instant the mental shock was almost more violent than the physical. Pros like Spaghetti don't shoot at the police.

Then Peroni realised he was being spun round like a child's top by a violent impact in his left hand. If Spaghetti had shot to kill, his aim had been off. The blood, however, was sensational.

Suddenly, as the spin came to an end, Peroni became aware of the sensation they had caused. The little orchestra outside Florian's had broken off in the middle of *Hello Dolly*; the pigeons were whirling skywards in a dark cloud; people were scattering in panic.

And Spaghetti had got clean away.

Further pursuit was out; Peroni was losing too much blood. He staunched it with a handkerchief, then went into the nearest bar, where he ordered a Chivas Regal and asked them to telephone police headquarters.

The wound wasn't particularly serious, but it involved a fair swathing of bandages and daily attention, so it was decided that Peroni should have a week off duty.

First, pure delight; he could scarcely remember when he had been off duty so long. Then the reaction went flat. What to do with the time?

In the end he decided to go and stay with his sister, Assunta, and her family in Verona. He and she had shared memories of a turbulent pre-adolescence in Naples. He was fond, too, of her jolly northern architect of a husband, Giorgio, and their two children, Anna Maria and Stefano. And it would be nice to go for trips to Lake Garda, drink Valpolicella and eat polenta and salame. But it was not to be.

'On Tuesday,' said Assunta, 'I'm going on a pilgrimage to

Assisi. May Day celebrations. Why don't you come, too?'

'A pilgrimage?' Peroni's ideas about pilgrimages were some six centuries out of date. 'But it would take more than my whole week off to get to Assisi on foot.'

'Don't be silly, Achille. We're going by coach. It's all organised by the parish, and I know there are still some places left. It'll be good for you, and you'll have a lovely time.'

Peroni took leave to doubt that. 'I'm not the sort of person for pilgrimages.'

'Nonsense – there's no such thing as a sort of person for pilgrimages. All sorts go.'

'Just the same I'd rather stay here.'

'Very well then,' said his sister. He was pleased, if surprised, at this unexpected surrender; Assunta usually never let go of an idea once she had got her teeth into it. 'The children can look after you. They're staying here with Giorgio. They thought it would be a nice opportunity to give some parties for their friends.'

'Parties for their friends?'

'That's right. They can never enjoy themselves when I'm here. I interfere all the time and make them turn down the music. So it seemed an ideal occasion. Giorgio will be chaperon. He doesn't mind teenagers dancing and playing music all over the house.'

'Perhaps after all it might be interesting to come to Assisi.'

'I thought you might feel like that. We leave at five o'clock sharp on Tuesday morning.'

The Woman in the Lime-green Coat

'Work on holiday?'

Peroni looked up from the file of documents he had been studying as the coach raced its pilgrimage along the autostrada. So, thought Assunta, might Agnelli look if interrupted in his perusal of the world markets on the way to the office in his bullet-proof car.

'This Camorra affair is remarkably complex. I can't afford to let myself get altogether out of touch with it.'

This conscientiousness will really have to go, thought Assunta. Her motives in organising the pilgrimage had been neither as pure nor as theological as her family thought. For some while now she had been noticing alarming symptoms in herself. She dozed in front of the telly, nagged the children mercilessly and never thought twice about letting Giorgio see her in curlers.

A similar process was taking place in Achille. Hitherto, she had always been the first to deplore the Neapolitan gutter-kid who lurked within her brother, waiting to snatch opportunities for depravity. But now things were going too far in the opposite direction. The *scugnizzo* was in danger of being smothered altogether, if he hadn't already been, and the Commissario was in complete control: conscientious, northern, self satisfied and, let's face it, dull.

While it was Assunta's intention to do something about this state of affairs, she had no illusions. She knew that a parish pilgrimage is not the most favourable of situations for awaking a throbbing past, but beggars can't be choosers, and if she had let this chance go by another might never have occurred.

So she had just a week to ignite a double miracle, and as of now she was keeping her eye cocked for even the most unlikely openings.

The coach turned off into the large forecourt of a Pavese grill which spanned the motorway. Up at the front their parish priest, don Sereno, whose cadaveric face had an expression of great sweetness, stood up and whispered into the microphone, 'A quarter of an hour for coffee, ladies and gentlemen.' He made it sound like a benediction.

The pilgrims started to stand up, some of them yawning and stretching, all looking slightly tousled. There were a lot of elderly women with the sort of hats that made you wonder whether their designers were motivated by a sadistic sense of humour, and a minority of men who looked as though they weren't quite certain what they were doing there in the first place. Not very promising material.

Then she noticed that her brother was looking up the coach with an expression she recognised well. Following the look, she saw that his attention had been caught by a woman in a lime-

11

green coat. And not surprisingly, for the woman was undoubtedly pretty, which was quite a thunder-clap in present company. A bit doll-ish, if you wanted to be critical. China-blue eyes which should have clashed with the coat, but somehow didn't. Blonde hair, fresh from the hairdresser. A just snub enough nose.

Could this be the opening? Achille had never, in fact, lost his interest in women, but Assunta had come to regard it as little more than the twitching of a corpse. Still, nothing was to be rejected out of hand. She would keep the woman in the lime-green coat under observation. And if she didn't, Achille evidently would.

'What are you looking at?'

Once that would have earned her a vulgar grin; it didn't now. 'Oh, nothing in particular.'

As they got off the coach and walked towards the main building, he continued to eye her surreptitiously. That lime-green coat must have cost a bit, thought Assunta. Nice legs, too, and Chinese porcelain ankles. Now what was a woman like that doing on a pilgrimage? Unaccompanied. She had certainly never appeared in church as far as Assunta had seen.

They followed her into the ground floor self-service store below the grill. With its regional wines, stream-lined cheeses, hams and salami, its luxuriously dispensable toys, the place was a temple to consumerism. Even the swishing roar of the autostrada was reverently hushed. They went up by escalator to the grill, and Achille watched the woman's legs.

'*Cappuccino*, please' said Assunta when they got to the top, 'and a packet of Marlboro.'

'But you don't smoke.'

'I *didn't* smoke.' She peeled off to the ladies before he could top that.

When she got back, Achille was stalking the woman, who was over by one of the windows. The lime-green coat was open now revealing a white cashmere jersey and a pleated grey skirt. Lucky to be able to wear it that tight, thought Assunta.

Achille moved in with the unobtrusiveness of an experienced hunter, and Assunta wondered what his opening would be. 'Is this your first pilgrimage to Assisi?' But maybe his sister's observation put him off his stroke for, at the last moment, he seemed to change his mind and came to join her at the bar.

'Your cigarettes,' he said, handing them to her. A hint of disapproval? He then ordered a cappuccino for her and an espresso for himself, and stood there drumming his fingers on the bar and failing to detain furtive glances at the woman in the lime-green coat. Assunta could almost see a question welling up inside him like a sob. She lit a Marlboro and waited for it.

'Assunta?'

'Um?' Here it came.

'Do you see that woman over there?'

'Which woman is that?'

'That one in the green coat.'

'Ah, that one – I hadn't noticed her before. Who is she?'

'That's – er – what I was going to ask you.'

'I've never seen her before.'

'But she's with us so she must belong to your parish.'

'It's a fairly big parish.'

'Strange, though, that you should never have seen her.'

'What are you so curious about?'

'Well, you might call it professional curiosity.'

There's a whopper if ever I heard one, thought Assunta. And then it occurred to her that there just might be a grain of truth in it as well.

'What's she doing here in the first place?' her brother went on, 'Alone.'

'Going on a pilgrimage to Assisi, like the rest of us.'

'But why?'

'Why is anybody else going? You, for instance.'

'That's just what I mean. There is an unusual motive for my being here. And I think there must be a fairly unusual motive for her being here, too.'

Assunta finished her cappuccino and meditatively spooned out the remaining cream froth. 'Achille,' she said, 'you're not suggesting, I hope, that there might be something – wrong?'

He considered the idea. 'I just don't know,' he said.

'On a pilgrimage of all things!' said Assunta. She sounded the correct note of shock, reflecting at the same time that the

13

pilgrimage had not started off too badly.

Peroni's interest in the woman was, he calculated, about three quarters amorous and the rest professional. She certainly promised to cheer up the pilgrimage, and he let himself daydream for several minutes about possible encounters. But then the Commissario intervened sternly, and he spent the rest of the journey studying his file on the Camorra.

Then around mid-morning their coach jolted into the crowded, medieval streets of Assisi and came to a halt outside one of its myriad hotels. From his seat, Peroni watched as she got up and made her way down the aisle towards the exit: a green-coated, lovely question mark. Then he got up to follow her.

But as he climbed out of the coach a sense of walking into the past struck him so forcibly that he momentarily forgot all about her.

Ever since he could remember, Peroni had had a capacity for getting onto the wave-length of the past, but it was something that he was both ashamed and slightly scared of, and when he had an attack of it, he grabbed for the nearest rational explanation. So now he put it down to the buildings. He had never been to Assisi before, and he hadn't been prepared for this extraordinary power of the architecture to propel you into the past. Venice had its stones, but they were nothing to this.

But unfortunately it was not only the stones. It was also a woman who happened to be walking by at that moment. She had long, black hair which fell down her back, and she was wearing medieval costume – a russet dress with the merest hint of a train behind. She seemed to be walking the streets of a city in which he was the intruder. He had the impression that if she turned and looked in his direction she wouldn't see him. He was a ghost in her world. But just the same he hoped she would turn round because he wanted to see her face.

Instead, with unexpected suddenness she rounded a corner and was gone. Peroni felt a wave of relief, just perceptibly mingled with disappointment, to find himself back among the twentieth-century pilgrims disgorging from the coach.

But where had she come from? He was beginning to feel an

14

uncomfortable shred of anxiety when the rational answer popped up at him like a jack in the box. Everybody wore medieval costume for May Day in Assisi. So that was that, and he hadn't had an alarming attack of the past after all.

Today, though, was only Tuesday and the May Day celebrations weren't till Saturday. Would somebody already be wearing costume?

Well, why not? In Venice Carnival used to go on all the year round.

But however neatly she could be explained away, a vision of the woman continued to linger hauntingly in Peroni's mind.

'Just time to check in and leave our things before we visit the basilica,' announced an eager-beaver pilgrim.

'Sightseeing before lunch?' Peroni groaned.

'A pilgrimage is a serious business,' said Assunta.

They checked in and Peroni, having dumped his bag, was coming out into the corridor when he spotted the woman with the lime-green coat once more. There were no doubts about the reality of her at any rate. She was at the head of the stairs with her back to him, apparently on her way back down to the lobby. Well, maybe she would like a Campari Soda at the cosy little bar he had noticed on the way in. He started to follow her.

There was something voluptuous about the way she walked downstairs, thought Peroni, and yet she had no idea she was being observed. Or did she? he wondered.

Circumstances seemed ideal. Lobby empty, bar glowing appealingly, pilgrims not yet foregathered. He quickened his pace.

But, instead of sitting in an armchair or going to the bar, she went to the desk and asked the smooth-faced receptionist something. He gestured with polite economy and she, nodding thanks, went in the direction of the gesture. A telephone booth.

Well, there was nothing so very odd about that. Natural enough she should telephone home to say she had safely arrived. Mother. Sister. Husband. Which?

Mildly put out but still optimistic, Peroni edged into a position where he could observe without being seen to do so. She picked up the receiver, and one fact slotted into place as he noticed the tell-tale mark where she normally wore a wedding ring. Then he watched her right index finger with its dawn-flushed nail move over the digital number composer.

The finger moved quickly, but not so quickly that Peroni could not count the number of times it pressed. Five. That was interesting because a Verona number with its prefix would have consisted of at least eight figures. So she was calling a local number: Assisi or thereabouts.

Peroni watched the soft skin of her jaw-bone in repose as the number rang. Once, twice, three, four, five times. No answer? Six, seven times. Then a sudden tension of the jaw-bone. A movement that corresponded with '*Pronto.*'

She spoke rapidly, obviously introducing herself, then paused. Impossible to say whether she was talking to friend or enemy, man or woman, but whoever it was, the business seemed urgent.

After a couple more seconds she began to speak again. She spoke for longer this time, maybe expounding the burden of her theme. Then she listened for a few seconds, spoke once more, briefly, and replaced the receiver.

Only possible to lip-read the final word: *Ciao.* That meant she was on second person singular terms with the person she had been talking to. Not that this revealed much.

She waited a couple of seconds in the booth. Most women did, Peroni had observed; probably to give them time to adjust their expression. Then she emerged.

Still time to make an approach. Peroni stepped towards her.

'Are we all ready, then, for our visit to the basilica?'

Peroni turned to see don Sereno smiling sweetly at the pair of them. If the old priest hadn't been so evidently overflowing with benevolence, Peroni could have throttled him.

'Oh yes, indeed,' she said with an expression of outrageous innocence, 'Quite ready. Oh, and by the way, Father, when are we going to visit the New Church? I've been told it's particularly interesting.'

'The New Church? Now let me see – yes, we're going there this afternoon. . . .'

She went off with don Sereno, chatting like an enthusiastic school girl. Whether or not she had been aware of Peroni's foiled

16

approach it was quite impossible to tell.

Talking of the Dead

'In the ferocious struggles that took place between the communes and city states during the Middle Ages it was not unknown for the relics of saints to be seized in armed raids. . . .'

Don Sereno's voice, so weak that Peroni had to strain to hear him, conveyed all the horror that he felt at the thought of such raids.

'For fear of losing the priceless remains of St Francis, the authorities of Assisi had a heavy armed guard kept on him – even during the period *preceding* his death. And some time afterwards, when the body had already been transferred here from the church of San Giorgio in 1230, Pope Eugene IV ordered the concealment of the coffin in which it was contained. . . .'

Peroni and his sister, the woman in the lime-green coat and the rest of the Veronese pilgrims were in the crypt, deep in the rocky guts of Mount Subasio beneath the crushing weight of the two churches, upper and lower, which together form the one basilica of St Francis, riding like a huge galleon into the lush green sea of the Umbrian plain.

'And so effectively was the secret of this hiding place kept that the body was considered lost for the best part of four centuries. Its rediscovery and scientific recognition only took place in the last century. . . .'

The place was packed with pilgrims whose prayer was so intense as to be an almost tangible force of which the dense copses of candles, flickering and flaring, were a visible expression.

In the very centre of this low, austere crypt was a great mass of grey stone clamped about with a wrought-iron grill, and in the front upper part of this mass was a sort of entrance through which you could see the heart of the whole vast basilica, the sarcophagus containing the crumbled dust of the little man from Assisi.

'You have to admit, though, we Italians are a bit kinky about

17

the dead.' Peroni spoke low, but not so low that he couldn't be overheard by the person standing immediately behind him, who happened to be the woman in the lime-green coat. Having had no luck with her so far he decided to see if he could get a shock reaction out of her.

'How do you make that out?' asked Assunta.

'Because quite contrary to our image abroad as festive children of the sun, we're really a nation of necrophiliacs. Look at the Venetians. Two merchants of Venice go trading in Egypt, and what is the supreme prize for which they risk death with the most appalling torture? The body of St Mark, which they conceal in a barrel of pork so that the Muslim customs men won't find it!'

'You can't count relics. They're meant to be a celebration of life, not of death.'

'All right then – take Dante. Having failed to burn him alive, they dug him up and tried to burn him dead. Then a friar stole the remains so as to stop the Florentines from doing so. And in eighteen something or other they dug him up again, and somebody stole a couple of bits which were sold for outrageous sums.'

He looked quickly at the woman in the lime-green coat. She didn't seem to be reacting much. He decided to increase the dose.

'Michelangelo – the Romans and the Florentines squabbled endlessly over his dead body, and it got stolen too. Paganini. He was left for years in a plague hospital because he was considered to be possessed, and then at last they got *him* up and buried him in Parma. And Christopher Columbus has got two tombs – nobody knows which is the right one.'

Looking back again Peroni saw that the woman was moving away. He might as well have saved his breath. What had promised to be the only bright spot in the situation was quickly turning into gnawing frustration.

'The niches you can see at the four corners of the crypt contain urns with the remains of Francis's four closest followers – Leone, Rufino, Angelo and Masseo – lying like faithful dogs at the foot of their master. . . .'

Peroni felt a kick of anger against the woman, his sister, the entire pilgrimage. He was a fool to have let himself be trapped

18

into it. He moved away from the Veronese group towards the stone steps which led up out of the crypt. Then just at the point where more steps go up to the right and to the left into the lower church, he halted before a small grille in the wall with a red light burning just inside it. He hadn't noticed this on the way down. For some reason he found himself staring at it, and as he stared he had another attack of the past. With all his rational mind he tried to pull himself back from it, but there was something dangerously attractive about the experience, as though he were having a secret assignation with a woman.

And then he noticed with some surprise that it was, in fact, a woman, for looking more closely at the grille he saw an inscription which said, '*Hic recquiescit Jacoba sancta nobilisque Romana*'.

Peroni had no Latin, but he knew that the first two words meant Here Lies. As they were in a crypt, of course, there was nothing very surprising about that. What was more baffling was the name. Jacoba? The final A made it indisputably a female name. What was a woman doing in such exclusively masculine territory? Come to that, what was anybody outside the circle, male or female, doing in a burial place reserved for the very core of the Franciscan movement – Francis himself and his four closest followers?

While he was puzzling about this he noticed that his fellow pilgrims, having finished with the crypt, were now making their way up to do some other part of the basilica. He took the opportunity to put the problem to don Sereno.

'Ah yes,' said the old priest with a smile of startling tenderness, ' "Here lies Jacoba, a saintly and noble Roman." The reference is to Jacopa – as she is more commonly known – de Settesoli, whose mortal remains are here enclosed. She was a rather unorthodox friend of Francis, being for one thing a woman and for another rich. Little is known of her. She was of the Roman aristocracy, and Francis jokingly used to call her "brother" Jacopa.'

Rather unorthodox. Peroni liked the sound of that, and for a moment he forgot the woman in the lime-green coat and went off on an impossible chase after this other woman whose dust lay behind the iron grille. What had she been like? Slim? Tall? Dark?

19

What colour had her eyes been? Had her hands been voluble, like those of so many southern women, or langorous? Had her voice been soft? Irrationally, he was quite unable to conjure up unattractive traits for her; if she was unknown, she seemed to insist on being alluringly unknown.

Then suddenly the image of the woman in the russet dress with the long black hair whom he had seen while getting off the coach walked once more in his mind's eye, and something stronger than reason insisted that she and this long dead Jacopa were one and the same woman.

These absurd meanderings were interrupted by a contemptuous and extremely vulgar sound. He was on the point of looking round to see where it came from when he realised that it had originated in his own chaotic private world. The author of it was his inner *scugnizzo*, who had been keeping so surprisingly quiet lately. Isn't there enough skirt among the living, whispered the implacable young-old voice, that you have to go chasing it among the dead?

And as though to emphasise the bawdy common-sense of this, a lime-green coat moved into Peroni's field of vision. The woman was making her way up from the vault.

He followed her.

A Superintendent of Fine Arts

As they emerged from the lower church into an open courtyard, poised between the two halves of the basilica, and halted there to make purchases at a sort of devotional supermarket, Assunta observed her brother hovering like an amorous dragon-fly in the region of the lime-green coat. An appropriately insect colour, she thought.

She herself was no nearer to finding the little door leading into the enchanted garden of lost youth. Probably, she reflected ruefully, it didn't even exist, and the whole pilgrimage was a silly waste of time, productive of nothing more than another adventure for Achille.

20

Detachedly she watched him as he prepared to descend on his prey. But just at that moment, as though calculating with minute precision, she moved off at a sudden tangent. Foiled again, dragon-fly, thought Assunta.

Purchases made, the party climbed up another stone stairway leading to the upper church, the walls of which, Assunta knew, were covered with Giotto's spectacular cycle of the life of St Francis – after Michelangelo's Last Judgement, probably the most stared at piece of painting in Italy. So it was with some surprise that she found the upper church looking more like a building site than one of the world's supreme tributes paid by art to sanctity.

The famous frescoes could still be seen, but only through complicated structures of scaffolding, draped here and there with canvas which badly obstructed the view. And in the middle of the floor was a large, gaping hole closed off with ropes.

'Oh dear,' came don Sereno's thin voice, 'I quite forgot to mention this temporary inconvenience in viewing the masterpiece of Giotto's youth owing to restoration work.'

'Restoration work?' said a cross-looking man who had been brought on the pilgrimage by his wife, 'Looks as though the place has been hit by a bomb!'

'The frescoes were gravely endangered as a result of earthquake damage,' explained don Sereno as if it were all his fault, 'and consequently drastic measures have had to be taken to ensure their safety. Fortunately,' he beamed at the brighter side, 'large portions are still visible, so I suggest we start by the door. Here you can see St Francis. . . .'

Assunta, who didn't like being shown around things, moved away to look at the hole in the floor. There was a man standing in it with his back to her and, as she looked at him, she had the odd feeling that she had seen him somewhere before. And with the feeling went an irrational, scary-exciting sense that something of moment was about to happen.

Then the man turned and she understood. Years had passed, but that irresistibly ugly face was unmistakable. It was a face which made you think that crookedness was much more interesting than regularity. The light that burned in the eyes, she remembered, looked as though it had been kindled in one of the more uproarious regions of hell. The face was now a deeply-scored labyrinth of lines which seemed to be in constant movement as though they were signalling his moods.

His name was Rocco Palanca, and a long time ago he and Assunta and Achille had swashbuckled and scythed about the slums of Naples. They had formed what had then seemed like an immortal trio and, although a constant duel went on between the two boys, they managed to maintain among the three of them a rough and ready alliance whose terms, if they had ever been put into words, might have been something not unlike One For All and All For One. From one second to the next she was out through the little door and into the enchanted garden. And once there, she found that she was head over heels in love with Rocco, just as she had been at fourteen.

She had never mentioned this love to him, and right up to the moment when they had been separated it had remained her secret. It still was. But whereas at fourteen she had been resigned to this, she now wanted to know more than anything else whether he had felt the same. Whether, perhaps, he still did feel the same.

'Rocco —' It was as though the name had been spoken by another woman.

He looked up with polite surprise and no recognition, which made her feel a fool. 'I'm afraid I don't —' he began, and then broke off. 'Assunta!' he said after a brief pause, 'What a delightful surprise!'

But something was wrong.

He climbed out of the hole and, ducking under the rope, gave her his hand. Cordial handshake.

'After all these years,' he went on, 'Well, well, well! And Achille?'

'Over there – trying to strike up an acquaintance with that woman in the green coat.'

'He hasn't changed, I see. I must go and say hello to him.'

As they walked across the nave together, Assunta felt more and more that something was badly wrong.

'Achille – how pleasant to see you.'

'Rocco, for heaven's sake – where did you spring from?'

22

And her brother's reaction, she realised, was not exactly that of one of the three musketeers meeting up with another after a lapse of years.

'I might ask the same of you.'

To her horror Assunta realised that they were talking pure Italian instead of the Neapolitan dialect they had always used together. But worse than that the two idiots were addressing each other with the formal *lei*.

'We came on a pilgrimage,' she said, hoping this would get the laugh it would certainly have deserved in the old days.

'Ah, indeed,' said Rocco, taking it quite seriously. 'Where from?'

'Verona,' said Peroni, and then, showing his bandaged hand, went on, 'I have a week's sick leave. I was involved in a little trouble.'

'Yes, I do seem to remember having read something about you. The – er – Clark Gable of the Italian police, isn't it?'

That proved he was posing, thought Assunta. He couldn't have made a mistake like that. When they were boys, he and Achille had made a cult figure of Rudolph Valentino. He had escaped from extreme poverty in the south to a fairy-tale splendour of wealth and fame just as they dreamed of doing. By then he had long passed into history, but for them his radiance outshone that of any king, and they fanatically dug up any detail about him they could find.

'Rudolph Valentino,' corrected Peroni, and the two men nodded like Chinese mandarins, taking that, too, perfectly seriously, 'And what about you?'

'As a matter of fact, I'm the Superintendent of Fine Arts here.'

Assunta felt that you could hear the capital letters.

'Really?' said Peroni, 'I seem to remember you were interested in pictures and that sort of thing.'

Assunta could only remember that he'd been interested in stealing pictures and that sort of thing, but she felt she would have shocked them both too profoundly if she had pointed this out, so she contented herself with saying, 'You used to call each other *tu*.'

'Yes, of course.'

23

'Indeed we did.'

There was an awkward pause as though they were now reluctant even to address each other for fear of having to use the second person singular.

Now Assunta knew what was wrong. The two men were suffering from the same complaint. Achille had become a Commissario of Police. Rocco had become a Superintendent of Fine Arts. They were Important Functionaries.

'Well,' said Rocco, 'I'm afraid I must be going. We have guests for lunch and my wife will be expecting me.'

The word 'wife' sounded like the tolling of a funeral bell in Assunta's ears.

'Perhaps we might meet again?' he suggested, not sounding any too eager about it, 'How long are you staying for?'

'A week,' said Peroni.

'Let me just look in my diary. Unfortunately it's a particularly busy period what with all this re-structuring work and one thing and another. Let me see. . . .' Even the diary with its gold pencil, Assunta noticed, was befitting a Superintendent of Fine Arts. 'I'm afraid today's quite out of the question, and tomorrow's as bad. Thursday no. What about Friday? I could manage lunch.'

'That would be splendid,' said Peroni with the tone of someone accepting a brand of laxative recommended by a chemist.

'One o'clock shall we say then? There's a quite reasonable little restaurant I often go to called the Excelsior.' Assunta groaned inwardly at the name. 'If you go to Santa Chiara, it's —'

'Oh, we'll find it,' said Peroni.

'Yes, of course – I was forgetting – a Commissario of Police should have no difficulty in tracking down a restaurant, should he?' The two men made dutiful displays of teeth at this exercise in wit. 'Well,' went on Rocco, giving his hand to each of them once more. '*Arrivederci.*'

'*Arrivederci,*' said Peroni.

'*Ciao,*' said Assunta, but there was death in her heart as she said the word, and it sounded like it.

Unexpected Development at a Stained-glass Works

Unmistakably package deal lunch. Pre-cooked spaghetti with meagre blobs of mince on top to justify the *alla bolognese* and now, with an uninspired inter-city hop, *cotolette alla milanese*, the greatest stand-by of cheese-paring restaurateurs.

'The lady over there.' Exuding innocent social perplexity, Peroni turned to the old priest who was sitting at their table. 'The one sitting right underneath the window. I know that I've met her, but I can't remember who she is. Can you help me, don Sereno?'

Assunta was on to him, he noticed, but that didn't really matter.

'Ah, you mean Signora Guidi.' The poor man was having trouble with his *cotoletta*. 'The wife of *Avv.* Guidi.'

'Ah, of course – that's how I know her!' Peroni looked enormously relieved. In fact, he was only telling a half lie because he did remember the lawyer vaguely from the days when he had been in Verona. An uninspired member of the forensic scene there and said to be a great medievalist. 'I didn't realise they were parishioners of yours.'

'Well, they live within the parish, though I'm afraid I've never seen them in church.' Don Sereno looked sad.

'And yet she came on this pilgrimage?'

'I confess I was a little surprised myself when she asked to join us. Then I thought that she must have a particular devotion to St Francis.' This possibility cheered him up a lot. 'A lot of otherwise non-practising people do, you know.'

'Yes, indeed,' said Peroni, thinking it was just about as likely that she had a particular devotion to higher mathematics.

The fruit had just been served – one sad apple each – when he saw her get up to go. He waited for a couple of seconds, then excused himself muttering something about a cigarette and also got up.

He threaded his way among the tables, smiling with the

25

professional charm of a diplomatic monsignore, and out into the lobby where she was sitting in one of the armchairs, having just lit a cigarette. There was something to be read in her expression, if only Peroni had been able to read it.

'Signora Guidi?' She looked up, not particularly interested. 'Forgive me if I introduce myself. I knew I'd seen you before, but I couldn't remember where. You were with *Avv*. Guidi at some ceremony at the Gran Guardia.'

He improvised with the exhilaration of an artist, knowing that no lawyer's wife in Verona could have failed to attend some ceremony at the Gran Guardia. 'Peroni,' he added, giving her his hand.

'*Piacere*,' she said, taking it and looking just slightly puzzled. Then the puzzlement cleared. 'You mean Achille Peroni?'

'That's right.' He waited for the explosion of feminine excitement which the admission unfailingly set off. It didn't come.

'How very interesting.' Three words.

'Would you like a coffee?'

'Thank you.' She would have said it in exactly the same way, he reckoned, if he had suggested a glass of cyanide.

He ordered two coffees and then tried again. 'What brings you on pilgrimage to Assisi?'

'I've always loved Umbria. So when I saw the parish was organising this pilgrimage it seemed just the thing – no worries, no driving, no journeys to organise.'

Peroni was familiar with the tone; he usually heard it when somebody was explaining how something had fallen off the back of a lorry.

She drank her coffee rapidly and then stood up. 'It was so nice meeting you. Thank you for the coffee.' She gave him her hand, then with a sweet but automatic smile was off and up the stairs.

Peroni stared after her. Behind the absent politeness he could sense powerful inner tension. The whole thing was both irritating and baffling.

It was also very intriguing.

She crossed the crowded Piazza del Comune and turned up into
Via San Paolo. Peroni waited until she was there, then set off in
cautious pursuit. The Commissario protested as he went: the
whole thing was grotesque and childish, the woman was free to
go where she pleased, and Peroni, not even in his own bailiwick,
had no right to follow her.

But he kept on walking.

Since their brief meeting after lunch he had not spoken to her.
During the afternoon, satiated with visiting things, he had
furtively cut loose and gone for one or two peaceful drinks in a
modern, non-cultural bar, missing, among other things, the New
Church in which Signora Guidi had evinced such interest. But
he had continued to brood on the puzzle she represented. And
then after supper, having looked about her to check that she was
unobserved (and not reckoning with Peroni's capacity for
surreptitious observation), she had slipped out of the hotel.

He had contemplated letting Assunta know what he was
doing, but she was strangely absorbed in her own thoughts.
(Something to do with the meeting with Rocco? He had always
half suspected she had been in love with him.) So after a mental
debate of about one second flat he had set off in pursuit of
Signora Guidi.

Via San Paolo was also full of people, so following unobserved
was no problem at all; and anyway, Peroni suspected, she was
far too caught up in her unknown enterprise to notice if a
platoon of *Carabinieri* had been following her.

But after a few minutes there were less people about and
Peroni fell back a bit and kept well into the wall, but the idea of
pursuit still didn't seem to enter her head, and she kept up a
brisk pace, not even glancing about her. She only hesitated
when she came to junctions, looking hurriedly at street names as
though she were following a route she only knew in theory.

The further they went, the more the crowd thinned out and,
at the same time, the character of the city about them changed.
The pinkish stone of the houses and the medieval (or deferen-
tially more recent) style of building were unchanged, but with
stubborn silence everything here announced that this was a
residential area. Even the moon, whitening the ubiquitous olive

27

trees, seemed to be private property.

Peroni could never put his finger on the exact moment when he began to feel that there was a third character on the scene. There just emerged in his mind an idea that may have been forming there for seconds or minutes.

The idea that he, in his turn, was also being followed.

But all his tests for detecting a follower were negative, so it had to be only an idea.

The street lighting was rarer here and Signora Guidi's pretty, shining head moved from brief, pale pools of light into long alleys of shadow.

'Belle! Arlette! *Piano – piano!*'

The squeaky voice from behind took Peroni by surprise, and he shrunk quickly into an archway, looking behind him. He saw a dwarf taking two dalmatians for a walk, or more accurately it was the two dalmatians which were taking the dwarf, for they pulled relentlessly, and he was dragged along behind with his little legs going like pistons, and as he went he kept calling out in a tone compounded of wrath and pleading, 'Arlette! Belle! *Piano!*'

This extraordinary trio raced up the street and past Peroni. Even Signora Guidi forgot her obsession for an instant and looked behind her to see the oncoming charge, but the dwarf and his dogs seemed to be unaware of anything or anybody outside their own little world, and continued their helter-skelter course up the street.

Then a few yards further on, and just before they drew level with her, Signora Guidi stopped, apparently having recognised her destination, and after a brief hesitation went in through a doorway. Peroni waited till the dwarf and his dogs had rushed past and then walked up to the building she had entered.

The first thing he saw was a large window, above which were the words FLORIO-LEVI VETRERIA. So Signora Guidi had most improbably gone into a stained-glass window shop, or more probably, by the look of it, a place where stained glass was made. For by the scarce light inside the window some of the products glowed dimly. The entrance was on the far side of this window with the door set back from the street.

Peroni looked in and saw no sign of Signora Guidi. She had been swallowed up by the stained-glass works.

Suddenly he lost patience with the whole business. Enough was enough. From now on he intended to frog-march all thoughts of Signora Guidi out of his mind and concentrate for the rest of the week on being a good pilgrim.

He turned and set off walking swiftly back towards the hotel.

Assunta lay on her bed after lunch the following day allowing her feet to throb in peace (the pilgrims had been doggedly visiting all morning), half listening to the radio which was incorporated into the head of the bed and thinking about Rocco.

She was crazy, she tried to convince herself, to resent the transformation of an ugly Neapolitan delinquent who she happened to love into a dignified Superintendent of Fine Arts who she didn't. It was the process of growth, and rebelling against it she was rebelling against life. A man might be pardoned for making such a stupid mistake because men didn't understand the workings of life, but for a woman there was no excuse.

Sunk in these thoughts, it came through to her slowly that the radio was saying something of interest. She started to listen, at first casually, then with an acute sharpening of attention. When it was done, she jumped off the bed and went to her brother's room down the corridor. She knocked.

'Avanti.'

He was reading. 'A guide book,' he explained. 'I was doing a little homework on the places we're going to this afternoon.'

'Never mind that,' she said impatiently. 'There was a murder in Assisi last night – probably not far from us. A man was shot.'

He looked up from his guide book quickly. 'What man?'

'The radio didn't say much about him. Just his name. Florio-Levi.'

Accustomed as she was to her brother's unpredictability, even Assunta was not prepared for the violence of his reaction to this news.

29

Enquiries of a Marxist Policeman

To those of his colleagues at the *Questura* or police headquarters in Perugia who didn't share his political views, Commissario Sergio Zanetti was known as Stalin. This was unfair because Zanetti probably believed far more sincerely in Communism than the Russian dictator had ever done. He was always trying to make life fit into the mould of Marxism, and although this was sometimes difficult, he never gave up trying.

So now as he examined the body of the good-looking young man with the massive blood-stain on his denim shirt where the bullet had entered, while missing nothing professionally, he wondered at the same time what the political motivation would turn out to be. Not direct political motivation such as terrorism, of course, but the indirect political motivation which was behind all human conduct.

The mere setting of the crime was indicative. Assisi was one of the greatest reactionary strongholds in Italy with an inflated artificial economy and a capitalist tourist trade based exclusively on medieval superstition. And stained glass was one of the principal industries boosted by that superstition.

On his arrival at the Florio-Levi works at eight thirty-seven that morning a modestly well-dressed woman with a sensible expression and an efficient air was waiting for him at the entrance. She must have been about forty, but she looked younger, and she was by no means unattractive.

It was a perpetual thorn in Commissario Zanetti's emotional flesh that so few good-looking women were militant Party members. Marx, he might have paraphrased, gets the women that men don't want, and the sheer injustice of it galled him. He thought that maybe, at a more appropriate moment, he might open an exploratory political dialogue with her.

'Bonato,' she introduced herself, giving him her hand, 'Raffaella Bonato.'

'Zanetti.'

'I'll show you the way.'

Her self-control under the circumstances, unless it was an act, showed promise of coherent political thinking.

Following her into the building, Zanetti and his team had the impression of moving into another world. They were in a chaotically untidy room which looked about the size of a fair-sized railway station. Doors led off it in all directions like entrances to corridors in a burrow, and at the further end a flight of wooden stairs led up to a sort of gallery. There were several heavy wooden tables covered with materials which Zanetti presumed were used in the production of stained glass. Countless sketches covered with scribbled indications, presumably directions concerning colour, hung crookedly around the walls, and in one corner there was a massive stone furnace, unlit, with a variety of rods and shovels and other instruments clustered hectically about it as though they were all trying to push their way in. Everything was very dusty, and there was an all-pervading acrid smell which tickled unaccustomed nasal membranes so that two of Zanetti's colleagues had already started sneezing. And everywhere there stood or lay sheets of glass of all shapes, colours and sizes.

Zanetti was wondering why the place was so deserted when the woman called Raffaella Bonato, as though she had guessed his thought, said, 'I sent the workmen home for fear they might inadvertently do something to hinder the police enquiry.'

'Very sensible.'

'He's in here.'

She had halted at one of the doors at the back of the works. It was just ajar and Zanetti, pushing it open, went in to find himself in a very small entrance with an old-fashioned hall stand complete with mirror. The door leading off this was also not quite closed. It opened into another room which was obviously a young person's living room-cum-study. There was a window looking out on some olive trees and a small church tower in the distance. In front of this was a big untidy desk surrounded by books, and beside this lay the young man's body. Apart from the denim shirt, he wore jeans and gym shoes. He was romantically good looking even in death. Black hair, full almost girlish mouth, Greek nose.

31

The faintest stippling of beard, only just out of the merely unshaven phase, gave him a vaguely Renaissance air, and he had one gold ear-ring in his right ear. His appearance strongly suggested bourgeois reactionary motives for his death.

After fundamental preliminaries, he turned to the woman once more.

'You found him?'

'Yes.'

'You live here?'

'No, I'm the firm's secretary. I got here at five to eight as I do every morning. He had asked me to call him. So I went and knocked at the door of his flat. There was no answer. After knocking a couple more times I went in and – found him lying there.'

'I see. Just exactly who is he then?'

'Lorenzo Florio-Levi.'

'Ah, so he ran this place, did he?'

'No. He was at university.'

'The son of the family?'

'Yes. The firm has been run by the Florio-Levi family for nearly two hundred years in Assisi. His father was the last.'

'You say was?'

'Both his parents were killed in an aeroplane crash three years ago.'

'Who runs things now?'

'Officially the head of the firm is Signorina Ermengilda Florio-Levi, Lorenzo's aunt, but she's been in poor health for some years. The actual production of glass is looked after by the man who used to be foreman. I am responsible for the business side.'

'So young Florio-Levi was alone in the building last night – except for whoever killed him?'

'No. Signorina Ermengilda also has a flat here. Above this.'

'But somebody could have come in here last night without her seeing them?'

'Oh yes. The two flats are completely independent.'

'And does Signorina Ermengilda know — ?'

'Yes, I told her immediately. She'll be expecting you.'

'Thank you. I'll see her immediately, but first there are one or

32

two more points I should like to clear up with you. When did you last see Florio-Levi alive?'

'Yesterday morning.'

'Was he in any way concerned or alarmed?'

'No, if anything the contrary.'

'Can you be more explicit?'

'He was always – well, enthusiastic. What you might call an effervescent sort of person. But just lately he seemed to be more than usually excited.'

'Any idea of the reason?'

'I assumed it was something to do with a woman.' She paused a second. 'It usually was.'

'He had many relationships with women?'

'I have no details of his private life. I just know he liked women and they liked him.'

'And you believe that the excitement he displayed recently was caused by one?'

'It would be natural, wouldn't it?'

'You've no idea who the woman might be?'

'None whatsoever.'

Zanetti looked about the room. Decadent pictures. Large collection of jazz records. Frivolous looking books. Then he noticed again the desk which one of his colleagues was going over at that moment, surrounded by books of an altogether more serious appearance. Excusing himself briefly with the secretary, he went over to the other policeman.

'Anything?'

'Just this.' A desk diary. The second policeman opened it at the previous day and indicated a single word entry.

Elisa.

'Do you know any Elisa he was friendly with, Signorina?' Zanetti asked.

'No.'

'It's the only mention of her,' said the other policeman in a professionally low tone, 'and there's no Elisa in the address bit at the end.' Zanetti looked through this with rapid attention. There were at least half a dozen female names with addresses, telephone numbers or both on every page.

'We'll take this back to the *Questura* and check on all of them. But first we must trace this Elisa.'

Then he looked at the books on the floor which had attracted his attention. He picked up one or two and glanced through them. Medieval history: unbridled reaction. 'Do you know what he had all these books for, Signorina?'

'He was at university in Perugia where he was writing some sort of thesis. I think the books were for that.'

'I see.' The typically useless knowledge disseminated in the fascist dominated universities of the west.

Then he noticed a skull half buried amid the confusion on the desk which his colleague had been sorting through. 'What's this?'

'It's a *memento mori, dottore*. Monks used to contemplate them to remind themselves of their own death.'

'Whatever did they want to do that for?' He turned back to the secretary. 'I'll speak to Signorina Florio-Levi now.'

The room was a stained-glass cave. The glass was fixed all around it except for the space in front of the two doors, and artificial lighting between it and the wall made it glow with extraordinary richness.

Commissario Zanetti did not appreciate the spectacle. For one thing, he found the biblical nature of it intensely irritating, for another, it represented a deplorable display of bourgeois personality cult. The best comment, he decided, was to ignore it.

'You're quite sure that you're real, I suppose?'

That was harder to ignore. Signorina Ermengilda Florio-Levi was a composition of extremes. She was dressed from head to foot in black – whether in mourning or not there was no telling – but her skin had the whiteness of a corpse or a clown, heightened by the cardinal scarlet of her mouth and nails, the sea-grotto blue of her eyelids and the brilliant dyed red of her hair. The artificial jewellery with which she was laden glittered in the light from the stained glass. She was seated in a revolving armchair which she rotated every so often so as to change her view of the biblical scenery, and in her hand she held a large glass of water.

'I beg your pardon?'

'I asked if you were real. Since you were brought up here by

34

Signorina Raffaella, I presume you are, but I have to be careful.'

She drank from her glass, and Zanetti realised that the contents were not water, but gin. He decided he must get control of the situation.

'Zanetti,' he said, 'from the *Questura* in Perugia.'

'Ah yes – Signorina Raffaella mentioned something. And you certainly look real enough. You'd better sit down.'

The furniture was tattered and none too clean. Zanetti, who was fastidious about his clothes, chose the least dusty looking seat, and resisted with some difficulty the temptation to spread out his handkerchief before sitting.

'I'm enquiring into the death of your nephew.'

'Yes, she mentioned that, too.'

'You don't seem particularly disturbed, if you don't mind my saying so.'

'We all have to die.'

'But he was shot last night in the flat below yours!'

'The manner, place and time of the crossing are of little consequence.'

'Did you have no feelings for him at all?' Even as he said it, Zanetti realised that the question was unprofessional and, worse, completely apolitical, but she had exasperated him into it.

She looked for the answer unhurriedly in her glass of gin.

'I wouldn't say that,' she said at length, 'I have many feelings for Lorenzo. As a small boy I was very fond of him. It's just that now I know I shall see more of him.'

'I'm afraid I don't follow.'

'The dead visit me frequently. On the whole I find them far better company than the living.'

In any soviet country she would certainly be in a psychiatric clinic.

'Signorina Florio-Levi, I want you to think about last night.' It was doubtful whether she was capable, but as she had been the only person in the building apart from her nephew and the killer, he had to try.

'When did you last see your nephew?'

'When he came to say goodnight to me last night.'

'What time was that?'

'I put no store by time. It's an over-rated and inaccurate system of measurement.'

Zanetti bit back abuse; it wouldn't have done any good. 'How did he seem?'

She examined the previous evening. 'Much as usual. Much as usual.'

'Wrought up? Excited?'

'Excitement was endemic in him.'

'Did he say he was expecting anyone?'

'Not that I recall, but I don't always recall everything.' She thought for a second. 'Sometimes I don't even listen.'

'When did he leave you?'

'Who can say?'

'But he did leave you shortly afterwards,' Zanetti found he was almost pleading with her, 'and that was the last time you saw him?'

'In the body.'

'After he had left you, did you hear anything at all from downstairs?' Once again she looked deep into the previous evening, and finally announced with solemnity, 'The bell.'

'What bell was that?' asked Zanetti, fully expecting some trans-stygian campanology.

'The door-bell, of course,' she said, suddenly practical, and taking him right off balance.

'Somebody calling?'

'That is the usual explanation, I believe, for the ringing of the door-bell.'

'Do you know who the caller was?'

'I scarcely think so.'

'Did you hear anything more after the ringing of the door-bell?'

This time she studied her crystal circle of gin, then thoughtfully drank some of it. 'Voices.'

'Whose voices?'

'Lorenzo's and a woman's'

'From up here you could hear them?'

'They were shouting.'

'Quarrelling?'

'Possibly.'

'Did you hear anything else? The sound of a gun?'

'No. I was rapt into another dimension.'

Zanetti took this to mean that she had gone to sleep, and imagined that even an American atomic explosion would hardly have penetrated her gin-soaked unconsciousness. With a leaden feeling of helplessness he tried once again to extract a time schedule from her, but this proved every bit as hopeless as he had expected.

'So some time after your nephew left you last night,' he concluded, 'the outside door-bell rang, and some time after that you heard your nephew quarrelling with a woman?'

'Much hangs on what you mean by some time.'

He knew it was the nearest he could get to confirmation.

'One more thing,' he said, 'Do you know of a woman called Elisa?'

'Elisa? Oh, but of course I do! Such a pretty little thing! She used to be one of Casanova's mistresses. She often comes to see me.'

Elisa at the Lesser Rock

Fortunately other developments made up for the severe mauling of frustration which Commissario Zanetti had received at the hands of Signorina Florio-Levi. At 1127 hours one of the men who had been making enquiries in the area returned to say that he had traced a witness who had seen a woman going into the Florio-Levi works at three minutes past ten the previous evening.

Given to extreme precision himself where time was concerned, Zanetti was not accustomed to it in others.

'Unusual for a witness to be so exact about the time,' he said.

'This is an unusual witness,' said the detective.

But even thus forewarned, he was taken aback when a dwarf walked into Signorina Raffaella's office, where he had established a temporary headquarters. The formal questions done, the dwarf, whose name was Amos Butturini, said he had been out walking the previous evening with Belle and Arlette.

'Belle and Arlette?'

'My dalmatians. And I challenge you to find two better trained dogs in Italy. I have my own command system based upon tone of voice, and it works with absolute —'

'I understand,' interrupted Zanetti, 'that you saw a woman coming into this building at three minutes past ten last night.'

'That's right,' said the dwarf, 'My quartz watch is infallible. Never a split second —'

'Can you describe her?'

'Fair-haired and probably blue-eyed, though I couldn't be sure of that with the light. About one metre sixty-two and fifty-five to fifty-eight kilos. Early thirties, wearing a lime-coloured coat and high-heeled shoes. Full lips, high cheek-bones and slightly snub nose.'

'How can you be so sure of all these details?'

'My observation is outstanding and I am famous for my memory,' said Amos Butturini a little huffily. 'Surely you've seen my television programme?'

'No,' said Zanetti, who only watched political transmissions.

'I know the *Divine Comedy* by heart and can recite it, backwards or forwards, starting from any —'

'Did this woman let herself in?'

'No, but she was obviously expected.'

'How can you know that?' asked Zanetti, irritated at the dwarf's apparent infallibility.

'Because the door was opened immediately. Somebody must have been waiting for her.'

'Can you tell me anything else about her?' Zanetti asked ironically.

Amos Butturini smiled complacently to himself. 'Plainly not from Assisi,' he said, 'as she was unfamiliar with her surroundings. Probably from the north. Reasonably well-off to judge from her clothes and handbag. Married, but involved in an extra-marital affair.'

'How do you make that out?'

'There was a certain furtiveness about her manner which a Signorina these days would not have, and no young woman going by night into a house where Lorenzo Florio-Levi lived could possibly be engaged on a licit affair.'

'You know the family then?'

'I,' said the dwarf giving the little pronoun regal stature, and fairly throbbing with self admiration, 'know everybody in Assisi.'

Two reports arrived fairly rapidly of people in the area who had heard what could well have been the sound of a gunshot. They couldn't be sure what the sound had been, but they roughly coincided over times. One said she had heard 'a cracking noise in the distance' just after turning the light out towards midnight. The other reported what he had thought was a car exhaust during a television programme which had started at eleven-thirty.

Then at 1452 hours, a policeman arrived with the gun. It had been found among some long grass in a field far down below a low stone wall overlooking the plain. The point from which it must have been thrown was only a few hundred metres from the Florio-Levi works. One shot had been fired from it.

Zanetti radioed the registration number through to Perugia, and at 1529 he was informed that the gun had been licensed to a certain *Avv.* Vittorio Guidi of Verona. He then had a check made through the scrupulously updated official records of hotel visitors in the town, and at 1616 he learned that a Signora Elisa Guidi from Verona had checked in with a party at the albergo Santa Lucia the previous day.

He telephoned the examining magistrate in Perugia who was handling the case and was given verbal authority to make an arrest.

At the albergo Santa Lucia he learned that Signora Guidi had returned to the hotel towards half past twelve the previous night looking extremely upset.

At the moment, he was then told, the Verona party was out sightseeing. Yes, as a matter of fact the receptionist did know where they were going that afternoon. They were going to the Lesser Rock.

Once upon a time there was an Assisi which had nothing whatsoever to do with St Francis. It was a pugnacious, gutsy little medieval commune, plundering and pillaging its way to prosperity, no better or worse than half a hundred like it up and down the Italian peninsula.

Today this almost unimaginable Assisi can best be perceived in the two fortresses without the walls known as *la Rocca Maggiore* and *la Rocca Minore*, the Greater Rock and the Lesser. The Greater is the one that draws the crowds, and on sunny days they swarm over its medieval masonry like locusts over the body of a prehistoric monster, for the most part unaware that what they are swarming over is an understudy monster. The original was built by the Emperor Barbarossa in 1174, and such were the horrors perpetrated there that the people of Assisi – Francis among them – literally razed it to the ground twenty-odd years later. The building where you eat your sandwiches today was built by the papal legate, Cardinal Albornoz, in 1367.

Peroni and the other Veronese pilgrims had climbed as much of it as their legs were up to that morning, and he had been able to observe that Signora Guidi was in an alarming state of nerves, smoking continually, biting her lip, kneading with her fingers and not taking a blind bit of notice of the Greater Rock.

Then after lunch had come the news of the murder at the stained-glass works, and Peroni had been pitched into as tormenting a dilemma as that of the donkey placed equidistantly between two bundles of hay.

After a brief hesitation he had told Assunta of the previous night's events, and had been greatly taken aback at her reaction.

'What are you laughing at?'

'Sorry. It just struck me that a situation like this is just what you need.'

'I fail to see why. And anyway, what am I to do?'

'Maybe it's a different Florio-Levi.'

'With a name like that?'

'Wait and see.'

'I can't just sit around doing nothing!'

'Why not?'

'Because I'm a policeman!'

'Well, you can't very well go out and arrest her either, can you? This isn't your territory – the police in Assisi will be handling it.'

'Perugia – Assisi comes under Perugia.'

'Perugia then.'

'Yes, and that's another thing. An enquiry will have started, and morally I can't withhold what I know from the police here.'

'Well, if your moral behind is itching as badly as that, go and tell them.'

'I don't want to.'

'Why not?'

'Because I don't want to go and throw the poor woman to the wolves!'

'Because the poor woman happens to be pretty. I bet you wouldn't have any moral scruples if it was one of the ones with funny hats.'

'The ones with funny hats wouldn't go round shooting people.'

'So you think she did it?'

'Strangely enough I don't. If Signora Guidi shot at someone, she would be mathematically certain to miss.'

'That's a male chauvinistic argument.'

'Well, I'm a male chauvinist. And I don't think Signora Guidi shot Florio what's his name.'

'In the circumstances, it's asking a lot to believe that she didn't, surely?'

'I know it is. She's obviously involved somehow.'

'So what are you going to do?'

Peroni thought for a second. 'I'll try and talk to her.'

But this he wasn't able to do immediately because the pilgrimage, having had a short rest after its package deal lunch, took off immediately for the Lesser Rock.

This much smaller edifice – a single tower and the remains of the outer wall – is in a privately owned field and attracts few tourists: if you've seen a tyrannosaurus why go out of your way for a minor predator?

When they arrived there, Peroni tried to get hold of Signora Guidi, but she stayed with the bulk of the party which would have meant hooking her out, so he put off the talk and went to look inside the tower.

There was a steep stone stairway in a dangerous state of disrepair, and either because of this or because the others had

41

had enough of historical buildings for the moment, he soon found himself alone. Helping himself with his hands, he scrambled to the top. Here, at the back of the tower, was a single bare stone chamber with a large window through which you could see Mount Subasio rearing towards its summit.

And as Peroni went into that room, the past sprang at him like a wild cat. It clawed him savagely, and as the attack did not come through the normal channels of the senses, he was unable to shake it off or even defend himself. He could only stand there, bearing the brunt of the feline onslaught, ignorant of what had happened in the chamber, but lacerated by the violence of it.

How long this lasted, he didn't know, but at a certain point he heard a sound behind him. The wild cat sprang back into its lair and, turning, Peroni saw Signora Guidi in the doorway. She couldn't have realised he was there, for she started and turned to go out. Peroni shook off thoughts of his mauling.

'Signora —' She halted unwillingly. 'Is there any way in which I can help you?' Coaxing tone. Neapolitan knight errant.

'What makes you think I need help?'

'Signora, observing people is my job, and even if it wasn't, I could still tell you were upset about something. I don't want to intrude into your private life, but if I can help you, I'll be glad to do so.'

She looked at him uncertainly. Traces of tears made her eyes look like rinsed forget-me-nots.

'It's very kind of you, but I don't see why I should bother you with my troubles.'

There was a hint of coquettishness even in her distress, as though she only intended to reveal her secret after having changed her mind about it a couple of times first.

'It's no bother to me, Signora.'

'What *good* can it possibly do?'

'Problems aired are problems shared.'

She hesitated a little more and then seemed to make up her mind.

'You see, the thing is I didn't come to Assisi to take part in this pilgrimage at all.'

'You didn't?' Peroni feigned thunderbolt astonishment.

'No, I came to Assisi because —' She broke off and bit her lip. 'I've been so silly you just can't guess, and I'm worried that —' She stopped again, then shook her head. 'No, there's no point in going through it all with you. You've been very kind and I appreciate it, but there's nothing you can do about it. I've been silly and I'll have to sort things out.'

She turned and went out. Peroni followed her, but without much hope of getting anything out of her now, and in fact she was already climbing inelegantly but purposefully down the steps. He watched her for a moment, then moved to a smaller window opposite the entrance to the chamber.

He could see the pilgrims way below sitting on the grass, walking about, talking. Then, after a while, he saw Signora Guidi's golden head emerge from the tower and stop as she got out a cigarette and lit it.

And then, looking towards the road they had driven up from Assisi, he saw a car stopping just behind where their coach was parked. Three men got out, and he had no difficulty in recognising them as policemen. After speaking briefly to the driver, they crossed the road and came down the path towards the tower.

The one who was obviously the senior of the three – bald, too neatly dressed, ascetic features, dissatisfied expression – went and said something to don Sereno. The old priest seemed to reel with consternation, then gestured weakly in the direction of Signora Guidi who seemed completely unaware of what was going on. The three men walked up to her.

Peroni was too high up to hear what they were saying, but he didn't need words to realise that she was being arrested.

A Pursuer of Rainbows

'You really must have your hand seen to today,' said Assunta. 'You don't want it to get infected.'

'No, I don't,' said Peroni. But his mind was on other things.

'Shall I pour you some coffee?'

43

'Thanks. May I look at the paper?'

She passed it to him. 'There's a picture on page one. She's certainly photogenic. Full story on page seven.'

After a bad night, Assunta had woken early and had time to go out and buy the paper before they started serving breakfast. Achille didn't look as though he'd slept any too well, either. Thinking about Signora Guidi. Well, that wasn't going to do either of them any good. The whole thing was clearly over now bar interminable legal proceedings and a life sentence which everybody except Signora Guidi herself would know perfectly well meant no more than twenty-five years maximum. Long enough, though, to turn her into an old woman.

The whole thing was sadly banal. She had met Lorenzo Florio-Levi during some sort of medieval history congress at Verona the previous year. The newspaper story didn't spell the situation out explicitly, but Assunta, who was on another deck of the same boat, could piece it together easily enough. Marriage to Veronese lawyer, older than herself, gone very stale. Encounter with exceptionally good looking younger man. Brief sojourn in heaven for her, casual lay on the side for him. And that should have been that. If the parish hadn't gone and organised a pilgrimage to Assisi. Immediately all Signora Guidi's frustrated passion was rekindled. Perfect opportunity for seeing Lorenzo again without her husband suspecting anything. What could be more respectable than a parish pilgrimage to Assisi?

Lorenzo Florio-Levi, not averse to a repeat performance, agreed to see her again. But when he realised that what she had in mind was something far more on grand opera lines – maybe an elopement – he told her unequivocally that he had no intention of singing that sort of duet. Humiliation, fury, bang-bang you're dead.

Compared with the QED solidity of that, her defence was pathetically thin. She had left her bag on a hall-stand in the entrance to Florio-Levi's apartment, and somebody must have removed the gun from it while she was in the living room of the flat talking with him. 'Talking' was the actual euphemism she used. Towards midnight they had had a disagreement and shortly after that she had left him, still alive. She didn't even realise that the gun had been removed.

'I wonder what she was carrying a gun for in the first place,' said Peroni when he had finished reading the story.

'I'm surprised at your saying that. You know better than I do that Verona today's worse than Chicago in the twenties. Giorgio makes even me carry one.'

'And what was Lorenzo doing at this congress in Verona?'

'Interested in medieval history.'

'Like her husband – he's said to be a medievalist. It's a coincidence. Well, let that pass. But if she really did shoot him – and shoot straight enough which, as I say, I doubt – would she just have gone on with the pilgrimage as though nothing had happened?'

'Why not? If she thought she was going to get away with it, it was the wisest thing to do. You said yourself she was very agitated.'

'Yes, but when I talked to her just before she was arrested yesterday, she said she'd been very silly. Now I don't think even Signora Guidi would have described murder as merely silly. And to judge by her expression when she was arrested, I don't think she even knew he was dead.'

'What was she in such a state about then?'

'Humiliation, shame, worry about the consequences.'

'You're wasting your time, Achille. Who else *could* have shot him?'

'The aunt, for example – Ermengilda Florio-Levi. The paper says she's got an apartment in the same building. Just as a hypothesis, she could have removed the gun from the handbag on the hall-stand while Signora Guidi was talking with the nephew in the living room, and then shot him after the Signora left.'

'She couldn't have known there was going to be a gun conveniently waiting.'

'No, she couldn't. Well, let's say that was a bonus. She planned to kill him anyway, then decided to incorporate Signora Guidi's visit into the project, so she went to eavesdrop on them and saw the handbag. Looking through it for something that would incriminate Signora Guidi, she found just the ideal thing – the gun.'

'Clever, but it's a bit like trying to explain a tummy-ache with some obscure Asian disease when the person's just eaten poisonous mushrooms.'

'I suppose it does seem a bit like that. What have we got this morning?'

'Eremo delle Carceri.'

'Well, I'll skip it. I'll walk to hospital instead and have my hand seen to.'

But Assunta had the impression that her brother's mind was still on other things.

The glass workers were intent on their craft. They moved slowly with bent heads, and made Peroni think of gnomes working precious stones in the heart of a mountain. They took no notice of him and he, uncertain of his ground, did not try to attract their attention.

'Can I help you?'

Pleasant, intelligent sounding female voice. Looking where it came from, he saw that the speaker fitted the voice. Not a beauty, but attractive. Grey-green tartan coat and skirt, white blouse, not quite flat-heeled shoes. To gain time, Peroni walked slowly towards her.

'I'm from the police.' A performance wouldn't have worked with this one. He showed her his police identity card, gambling that she wouldn't look closely enough to see that he was attached to the *Questura* of Venice. She glanced at it, then looked back at him.

'You'd better come into my office.'

She led him into a small room in almost comical contrast with the vast, dusty, higgledy-piggledy glass works. Here everything was neat, clean and in the place assigned to it. Letters and papers lay symmetrically in their trays, the typewriter had its cover on, half a dozen newly sharpened pencils stood to attention in a special holder. There were personal touches as well: a couple of photographs on the desk, a small vase of flowers, an attractively painted plate with Wolf Hotel written on it.

'Please sit down.'

Behind the polite exterior he sensed shyness. The right current

46

would have to start flowing between them if she were to talk naturally.

'A funny name for an hotel surely?'

She looked briefly taken aback, then glanced round at the plate and smiled. 'It's the Wolf Hotel in Gubbio,' she said, 'A nice place with a very good restaurant. I often stay there. It's named after the killer wolf which St Francis tamed. He – the wolf that is – spent the rest of his life peacefully in the town, and the citizens provided his food. It used to be fashionable to say that the whole thing was a pious legend and that the wolf was really a bandit. Then a few years ago they dug up the skeleton of an enormous wolf in Gubbio.'

'Really!' said Peroni, all eyes.

'Truly!' she said, 'I don't know which I like best – the story or the sequel. But I'm sorry – you haven't come here to talk about stories or hotels.'

'No, no,' said Peroni, who had achieved the effect he wanted, 'I find it very interesting.' He paused, slipping effortlessly into a confidential manner that never failed with women. 'My colleagues yesterday learned all the essentials and, as you know, an arrest has been made. I just want to fill in a little background.'

'I'll be pleased to give any help I can.'

The right current was flowing now all right. No longer policeman–witness, but two friends, each pleasantly aware that the other was of the opposite sex. 'To start with,' he said, 'what was Lorenzo doing up at this medieval history congress in Verona?'

'Oh, it was his subject. Even when he was a little boy he was passionately interested in history, particularly the middle ages. He was reading history at Perugia University.'

'Well, that clears that up then. Another thing: can you give me some idea of what sort of person he was?'

She considered the question carefully. 'Above all,' she said after a second, 'he was a romatic. Oh, I don't just mean as far as women were concerned. They liked him certainly, and he liked them, but I mean in a more general sense. Going back to his boyhood again, he was always getting wildly enthusiastic about crazy ideas. He never grew out of that – he liked doing silly, dangerous, exciting things.'

'In other words, he chased rainbows as well as women?'

47

'Very well put.' She smiled at him and he smiled back.

'Had he been after any rainbows recently?'

She frowned. 'That hadn't occurred to me. But to judge by the air of excitement about him – yes, he might have been.'

'Any idea what sort of rainbow?'

'None whatsoever.'

'When did you first notice this air of excitement?'

'Oh – maybe about a month ago.'

'Mounting or diminishing?'

'Mounting if anything.'

'Any particular incident strike you?'

'No. . . .' Then the hem of her memory seemed to catch on a nail. 'Wait a minute – it's nothing much, but it did strike me at the time. One afternoon about a fortnight ago he came in here and asked me to get him a train ticket for Rome the next day because his motorcycle was being repaired. I remember thinking at the time he seemed particularly elated, as though he were on to the final clue in a treasure hunt.'

'And when he came back from Rome?'

'I didn't see him for a couple of days after that, and when I did I'd forgotten all about it.'

'Can you think of any other way I might get a line on to this?'

'You might ask his aunt, Signorina Ermengilda.'

'Would you take me to see her?'

'Yes, of course. She's not in very good health though, and her behaviour can be a little strange. I think your colleague yesterday was a little – well, taken aback.'

'Yes,' said Peroni, adding another egregious whopper. 'He told me.'

Ilario the Rubicund

'You see that man there – bald and squatting on his haunches? That's my great grandfather, Tommaso Florio-Levi, as Jonah in the belly of the whale. He always put a self portrait in his windows. It was his way of signing a work. Not that he needed a signature – a

48

blind man could see that only Tommaso Florio-Levi could have managed to get so much colour into the belly of a whale. Look at the green of Jonah's tunic and the silver and pink of those fish and the shifting red cast by the candle flame, and notice the way that the rib-cage seems to be moving.'

'Extraordinary! Peroni had slipped unthinkingly into the role of disciple, and whether because of this or because of the gin he was sharing with Signorina Florio-Levi, he found himself appreciating stained glass for the first time in his life.

'Beneath that you can see Jonah sitting beneath his gourd waiting for the destruction of Nineveh. . . .'

His mind continued to tick over as he followed her through the biblical landscape jostling with prophets and kings and saints and sinners. He feared that he would get little from her of practical value. She was an alcoholic living most of her waking life in a private world of stained glass and shadows. Where did that leave her as a potential killer of her nephew? Obviously, she couldn't be ruled out, but Peroni had decided to by-pass that aspect of it for the moment on the grounds that the police in Perugia couldn't have altogether overlooked the possibility. He equally decided not to try and make her go through the night of the shooting. He would be unlikely to learn anything they hadn't already learned and it would consume too much time, a point which couldn't be overlooked in view of the possibility of the official enquirers taking it into their heads to pay a return call. He would concentrate instead on Lorenzo's rainbow in the hope of finding a crock of something or other at the end of it.

'Your nephew Lorenzo —' he began.

'Dead!' said Signorina Florio-Levi, 'Part of the great majority. Better that way. Gin.'

Peroni poured for her. 'He didn't follow in the family tradition?'

'The genius missed him. My brother, Eugenio, was the last of the line – the greatest line of stained-glass workers in Italy. Maybe if I had had a son. . . .' She stared through gin fumes at this unborn master craftsman.

'Lorenzo,' Peroni steered her gently back, 'before he died, in the last month of his life —'

49

'It's no good talking to me about time. I don't use it.'

'He was very excited about something, as though he were making some kind of discovery. Have you any idea what this might be?'

She was silent for so long that Peroni thought she had passed out, and it seemed doubtful whether the question had even got through to her at all. So he nearly choked on his gin when she uttered the single word, 'Ilario.'

'I'm afraid I don't quite follow.'

'It was his meeting with Ilario that stimulated him.'

'Who is Ilario?'

'A friend of Lorenzo's. A friend of mine, too.'

'Do you know his second name?'

She stared into the gin. 'I've never been told it.'

'Where does he live?'

'Here in Assisi.'

Questions and answers were flowing, thought Peroni, but where to? 'Do you know anything else about him?'

'He is a poet.' She pondered the statement as though it were a defective stained-glass window. 'A bad poet,' she added at length.

'When did Lorenzo —' Peroni began, and then realised the uselessness of the question. 'You say Ilario is a friend of yours, too,' he substituted. 'Where did you meet him?'

'Here. He came to see me.'

'What does he look like?'

This needed thought. 'Rubicund,' she said eventually.

There was a suspiciously stained-glass quality about the adjective, and Peroni wondered whether she might be making it all up. 'Did you ask Lorenzo why he was so excited about his meeting with Ilario?'

'I did. He said it was like a baby rabbit.'

'I beg your pardon?'

'What Ilario told Lorenzo,' she said with sudden exaggerated clarity, as though Peroni were a bit soft, 'was like a baby rabbit. Baby rabbits die if seen too young. Lorenzo did not wish to reveal what he had learned from Ilario for fear it would come to nothing.'

'And did you ask Ilario what it was all about?'

'I did.'

'What did he say?'

She made another lengthy pause, finished her gin and fixed Peroni with a glittering eye. 'He winked,' she said.

The room was very quiet as though it were recovering from the violence which had taken place in it the other evening and the subsequent ruthless stripping and mauling which it had been subjected to at the hands of the police. The only ostensible sign of the tragedy was the outline of Lorenzo's body over by the desk in front of the window, but for Peroni, who had a feeling for these things, every object screamed silently that it had been wrenched out of its customary routine.

Under such circumstances he was probably wasting his time here even more than he had been upstairs with Lorenzo's aunt; anything remotely of interest would have been taken by the police. But he stayed just the same.

A pleasant room. Comfortable, untidy, varied. He registered that the pictures would have appealed to his niece, Anna Maria, who was into trendy art having just started at the Liceo Artistico. And the jazz records would have scored with his nephew, Stefano, who, from intellectual heights, anathematised pop, but had a cult for jazz.

He turned to the books. A lot of history which squared with what the nice secretary had said, but other things, too. Chess, astronomy, cinema, astrology, poetry, zoology, philosophy. A young man with a questing mind and given to enthusiasms.

So what had his last enthusiasm been?

Peroni went over to the desk and surveyed the chaotic jumble of objects with some gloom. The police certainly wouldn't have let anything escape them here. Nevertheless, he started to sort through the confusion. One or two things raised private question marks of their own. What, for instance, was an alabaster owl doing there, no bigger than your thumb? And – emerging suddenly from beneath a heap of paper as though the last trump had that very minute sounded – a skull.

It grinned at Peroni tauntingly. Then as he reached to pick it up he had the impression that it was baring its teeth to bite his hand. But it let itself be picked up without resistance.

Peroni contemplated it. It was fixed on a wooden pedestal where it must have stood grinning at Lorenzo. What did a young man like him have a thing like that for? The skull was uncommunicative. I'm not saying anything, it seemed to sneer, and you won't guess the secret. Assuming there is a secret to guess. You're as dumb as I am.

He put it down again and looked at the piles of books on the floor. Could they have something to say? He picked up one or two. Medieval history. Nothing new there. He moved the books about a bit, glancing at titles here and there, and then unexpectedly one caught his attention.

It was scarcely more than a pamphlet, and it was in French, dated Paris 1899. *Frère Jacqueline* by E. d'Alençon. Odd to find the word brother attached to a female name. And then Peroni realised that this was not the first time he had heard of such a thing. In the basilica the day before yesterday, don Sereno had said that Francis referred to Jacopa as brother Jacopa. And come to think of it, Jacqueline was probably the nearest thing you could get in French to Jacopa.

Peroni opened the booklet. His French was rudimentary, but it was sufficient for him to be able to understand, with an illogical catch of excitement, that it was indeed about her. So Lorenzo's medieval studies took in Jacopa de Settesoli. She was, of course, a medieval figure, but that didn't prevent Peroni feeling that, if only he could get at it, there was special significance here.

But further leafing through the books revealed nothing more, and he began to think that, in spite of the windfall of coming across Jacopa in that learned company, he was no nearer to Lorenzo's rainbow. He was on the point of packing up the search altogether when he glimpsed, wedged between books and desk, a notebook. He got it out.

A reporter's type notebook with a spiral hinge. Opening it, he saw a hurried, untidy handwriting which fitted exactly with what he knew of Lorenzo. History notes, probably taken at lectures. A great deal about quantitative history which had Peroni puzzled for a while, but transpired to be the examination of human affairs through wills, bills and similar everyday documents, as opposed to qualitative history which concerned kings, wars and political skulduggery in general. Interesting, if not necessarily to the point. He leafed through the notebook without finding anything to take him any further. Quantitative history was, he realised, exactly the same as police work: ultimately the stuff of reality, but taken piece by piece repetitive and soul-destroying. And then a name jumped up from the notebook and gave him the mental equivalent of a karate chop.

ILARIO IL RUBICONDO.

Written in capitals and boxed off with four lines. So Signorina Ermengilda had not been leading him up a stained-glass garden path after all.

Or had she? For immediately underneath the name was written 'Town crier of Assisi 1218–1240.' And when she had asked him what it was all about, he had *winked* at her? However, the main thing was that a rubicund Ilario had existed. The first real indication.

He read on, deciphering the helter-skelter handwriting with some difficulty. 'Chronicles. Worse kind of doggerel verse. V. scurrilous. Purporting give news re people, events in A. when I. was town crier. Often pleb gossip or fruit of I's imagination. Crude idea of life in A. 13th c. Pop. of A. – friars included – all sodomites, simoniacs, adulterers, panders, thieves etc. Chronicles mostly transmitted by word of mouth among pop. No complete edition exists. Frequently quoted by contemporary and subs. authors. Anon. A. scholar 19th c. made largest known coll. Missing.' This was followed by a peremptory imperative in block capitals and underlined three times. TRACE.

A line was then drawn right across the page, and this was followed by two addresses: Via Pozzo della Mensa 12, and Via Borgo Aretino 35. Nothing more was written in the notebook. Peroni copied out the addresses, concealed the notebook where he had found it and left.

As he emerged and crossed the floor of the works, one or two of the gnomes, presumably having learned he was a policeman, looked up from their work and followed him with their eyes.

He knocked on the door of the pleasant secretary's office.

'Have you ever heard of somebody called Ilario il rubicondo?'

53

he asked her when he was inside.

'Oh yes,' she said, 'Lorenzo was going to do his graduate thesis on him.'

'Going to? He hadn't started writing it?'

'No, he was still researching it. About a week ago I offered to help with the typing, and he said he didn't plan to start writing until the autumn.'

So it looked as though that hopeful little track was a cul de sac. Unless Lorenzo had managed to trace that anonymous nineteenth century collection of Ilario's Chronicles and found there whatever it was that had so excited him. 'Lorenzo did not wish to reveal what he had learned from Ilario for fear it would come to nothing,' Signorina Florio-Levi had said.

'The Signorina,' he went on, 'told me that she knew this Ilario, that he was a friend of hers and of Lorenzo's.'

'Probably Lorenzo talked to her about Ilario and she, being so much alone in that apartment, continued to think about him until he became a real figure for her. The border between the real and the unreal is not very clearly marked in her mind.' Unexpectedly she smiled. 'Though often the people who think they can see it most clearly marked are the ones who are most mistaken about it.'

'That's true, too.' He smiled back at her, then showed her the two addresses. 'Do either of these mean anything to you?'

She looked at them and shook her head. 'No – I mean they're both in Assisi, but I've no idea who lives at either of them.'

'Can you tell me whereabouts they are?'

She brought a map of the city round to his side of the desk and, as she bent down to show him the two streets, he felt her hair brush quickly against his forehead and he reflected that the man who got her would be lucky.

Through the Door of Death

There is a tradition which explains the existence of the doors of death such as the one Peroni was now looking at. Most of the medieval houses in Assisi have these doors. They stand about a

54

metre above pavement level, and during the Middle Ages they were only opened for carrying out corpses. The tradition says that this was to symbolise the fact that the soul of the dead man, who had entered the house by the normal door, now remained behind his body with the family as a sort of household god. Today the doors of death are mostly bricked up.

But this one had been adapted to serve as the main entrance to the house. The job had been tastefully done so that not even Rocco in his official capacity could have raised any objection. Three steps of locally quarried stone, in perfect keeping with the rest of the house, led up to it, and the wooden part was obviously authentic, and yet the effect was as shockingly anachronistic as an ancient coffin used for a window box.

Via Pozzo della Mensa, the first of the two addresses Peroni had found in Lorenzo's notebook, was a narrow medieval street, bright with geraniums and abundant in archways, and this particular little grey stoned house would have been in perfect harmony with the rest of it if somebody hadn't called back to life its door of death.

With an odd sense of reluctance Peroni climbed the three steps and rang the discreetly gleaming bell.

The door was opened by a dragon in maid's uniform who looked at Peroni as though he'd come to sell her a fire extinguisher. '*Si?*'

'*Questura.*' It seemed to Peroni as though there were a flash of something not unlike alarm, but if there was, it went as quickly as it came.

'I'll tell Signora Rosalba. Please wait here.'

She lèt him pass into the hall and then proceeded, after knocking, into a room leading off it, closing the door behind her. Peroni looked about him. He saw at once why the door of death had been opened; it gave the hall more space and symmetry. It just happened to be wrong as well. Everything about him was in perfect taste, and at his feet there glowed a banked fire of Persian fantasy, but there was the same sense of wrongness as there had been about the door. The personality of the house had been subtly, expensively and exquisitely outraged.

'Signora Rosalba will receive you.' She moved very silently for

55

a dragon.

She held the door open, and he went in. Taste and expensiveness were unwavering, and the woman who now rose from an embroidery frame to meet him, needle in hand, went with the interior decoration. Via Veneto elegance. Discreet sapphires. Fair hair apparently fresh from the hands of the sort of *parrucchiere* you wouldn't find in Assisi. White dress of couturier-styled simplicity. Make-up a work of art. But, like the house, there was something wrong.

Peroni didn't have time to speculate about what it was, though, for after dismissing the dragon with a murmured 'Thank you, Emma,' she gave him the second shock of the visit by saying, 'May I see your police identity card, please?'

Hoping she wouldn't notice the Venice discrepancy, he passed it to her. She examined it carefully, and Peroni scrabbled in his head for a justification to give if challenged. Only just transferred, new card not issued? But then with a smile that went with her appearance she handed it back to him. Very feminine, he thought, to make such a point of checking credentials and then not notice what's wrong with them.

'Do sit down.'

'That's a remarkable piece of embroidery.' It was, too: two birds of paradise against a background of exotic foliage.

She smiled a finely measured smile of acknowledgement. 'I've always been fond of embroidery. Can I get you a drink?'

To his surprise he accepted a Martini, a drink he didn't particularly like as a rule. Watching her make and bring it to him, he was put in mind of a very high-class geisha, a woman who knew how to do things to please. Like that embroidery. Accepting the Martini, which was delicious, he slipped into the role of male having his tummy tickled.

'What can I do for you, Commissario?'

He forced himself to concentrate. 'I'm enquiring into the murder of Lorenzo Florio-Levi.' Did that get a reaction? Her steady grey eyes didn't say anything. 'As you probably know, an arrest has been made, but there are one or two points that need clearing up. I came across your address in a notebook of his, and I wondered if he had been in touch with you.'

'Yes indeed.' A modest, economical but attractive crossing of legs. 'He called on me – let me see – rather over a fortnight ago.'

'You didn't know him before?'

'No.'

Peroni wondered what had happened at the encounter. He wondered, too, about her. Did she live alone, guarded by the dragon? She had no wedding ring, and there was no sign of a man about the house, but surely all that exquisitely tended femininity wasn't just wasted on the Assisian air? Emma had certainly referred to her as Signora, but that could have been honorary. Aloud Peroni said, 'Do you mind if I ask what he came for?'

'Not in the least. He came to see the house.'

Almost the last answer he would have expected. 'To see the house?'

'That's right. He asked me if I would show him over it. I obliged.'

'And that was all?' A silly question with a clumsy double meaning.

'That was all.' Quite undisconcerted by the implication of the question.

'Did he say why he wanted to see the house?'

'Yes. He said he was preparing a graduate thesis concerning Assisi in the Middle Ages, and this house interested him because apparently in the light of recent research it is believed to have been lived in during part of the thirteenth century by a well-known local figure. A woman called Jacopa de Settesoli.' Observing Peroni, her eyes widened perceptibly. 'Have I said something wrong?'

'No, no – you just took me by surprise.'

This was the third appearance that Jacopa had made on his mental horizon. First in the basilica with the little red light. *Hic recquiescit Jacoba.* . . . Then in Lorenzo's apartment Frère Jacqueline. And now this. Although he had no conception of how it could be so, he felt that she must be somehow involved, and because he was involved, too, this gave him an irrational sense of joy.

'So you showed Lorenzo over the house,' he went on, trying to sound matter of fact. 'And then?'

57

'And then he shook hands, thanked me politely and went his way.'

'That was the last you heard of him?'

'Until I learned of his death.'

'He told you no more?'

'No.'

'No hint of anything that might have had some connection with his death?'

'No.'

'He didn't by any chance mention another thirteenth century character, an Assisi town crier named Ilario il rubicondo?' She shook her head. Peroni changed direction. 'Could you tell me in what manner he went over the house? I mean, did he examine it room by room? What impression did he give you?'

'He went over it very thoroughly indeed. To tell you the truth, I had the impression he was looking for something more than material for a thesis.'

'But he gave you no clue as to what?'

'None whatsoever. And if he *was* looking for something the poor boy was wasting his time. I had the entire place done over when I moved in last winter.'

What it was all about, Peroni reflected, there was still no telling, but there were beginning to be indications that it was about something more than a brief encounter with Signora Guidi. He got up. 'You've been very kind.'

'Not at all. I wish I could have been of more help. I'll get Emma to show you out.' She touched a bell-pull. 'Oh, by the way,' she went on, 'Saturday, as I daresay you know, is May Day and there are great festivities here in Assisi. I'm giving a small luncheon party for the occasion, and I should be extremely pleased if you could come.'

He felt less enthusiasm than such an invitation from such a woman would normally have aroused in him. It must have been the house. But it would be silly to refuse. 'Thank you very much.'

'Any time around luncheon.'

The dragon named Emma materialised soundlessly. 'Signora?'

'Please show this gentleman out, Emma.'

When he was at the door Peroni remembered the second

address in Lorenzo's notebook and turned back. 'Via Borgo Aretino 35,' he said. 'Does that address mean anything to you?'

Her forehead wrinkled lightly with perplexity and she shook her head.

'Nothing at all.'

Peroni followed Emma out. In the hall she opened the door of death for him, and with a curious sense of relief he walked through it and out into the street.

Reflections of a Literary Lady

The door of Via Borgo Aretino was opened to Peroni by an ageless and fluttering female with clothes of drifting stuffs which floated about her like tired wings. Her nervousness, apparent even in the way she peered out through the scarcely opened door, was reflected in these stuffs which never compromised themselves with a downright colour, but went in for hazy, indefinite browns and greys with occasional hints of the timidest of yellows and greens.

'Yes?' she said, making it sound like a plea for Peroni to be transported elsewhere.

'*Questura.*'

If he had produced a gun, the effect couldn't have been more shattering. She stared at him for a second with widened, terrified eyes, then slammed the door in his face. Even the sound of her running footsteps within conveyed panic.

Peroni waited, uncertain what course to take next, but before long he heard more footsteps, this time returning, and the door was opened again by the same female.

'She will see you now.' The first word of the sentence was given strong emphasis, and the tone was one of reverence.

Another she? thought Peroni as he stepped into the hall. The place could hardly have been in greater contrast with the one he had come from: everything was threadbare, shabby, disordered, and everywhere there were books which somehow gave the impression that they were given the free run of the house and wandered about it as they felt disposed, singly or in groups, settling where and when they wished.

'In here.' The whisper was even more reverent, and Peroni felt as though he were being ushered into the presence of the Pope.

The room he now entered, with its window looking out over the green sea that stretched towards Perugia, was plainly the capital city of the books. Here, seemingly in their thousands, they had taken over completely. There were volumes of every possible description: fat and thin, young and old, luxuriously bound and down-at-heel, ancient paperbacks on their last legs and tough looking dictionaries and encyclopedias. But though the take-over was indisputable, it was also evident that the books were amenable to peaceful co-existence, for perched or curled on various of their number – there was nowhere else to perch or curl – were some dozen cats, almost as various in character as the books.

And seated at what would have revealed itself to be a desk if you had been able to see a square centimetre of it for books and cats was the human viceroy of this bibliographic-feline commun-ity. She was a distinctive figure: grey hair cropped short, heavy black horn-rimmed spectacles on Roman nose, jutting chin, tweed jacket, shirt and hand-woven tie. Her lower parts were invisible, being submerged in cats and books. At the moment of Peroni's entrance she was typing something, a Tuscan cigar between her teeth and the stubs of its predecessors in an ashtray on her right.

With some difficulty she struggled to her feet, held out her right hand to crush Peroni's and barked the single word 'Higgins.'

'Dame Iolanthe Higgins,' corrected the first female, who was fluttering at the door.

'Stuff, Alice! Police haven't got time for standing on ceremony.'

'Peroni,' said Peroni, completing the introduction.

'Alice, get a chair for the Commissario.'

Apparently miraculously, Alice produced a chair and sufficient floor-space for Peroni to use it.

'Perhaps a cup of tea —' she then began in a quavering voice.

'Cup of tea be damned!' roared Dame Iolanthe, 'I wish you'd get cups of tea out of your head once and for all. Bring us the whisky and two glasses.'

'But the doctor, Iolanthe —'

'Damn the doctor, too! Old womanish quack!'

'But, Iolanthe, your blood pressure —'

'And damn my blood pressure! That makes three. Are you going to get the whisky or are you not?'

'Yes, dear —'

'Then go and get it!'

It was the accent, amongst other things, which fascinated Peroni, for while the two women spoke together in Italian, they were both unequivocally English.

'So,' the Dame continued, 'You've come to see me about young Florio-Levi. Can't say I'm surprised – matter of fact, I was expecting you.'

'How is that?' asked Peroni, trying not to sound as surprised as he felt.

'I'm not a crime writer for nothing – I know how you policemen's minds work. You don't leave stones unturned.' She inhaled heavily on her Tuscan cigar and collapsed in a helpless, spluttering fit of coughing. 'Damn this cough!' she roared when she had partially recovered, 'Alice, where's the whisky? Yes,' she went on to Peroni, 'you don't leave stones unturned, so I guessed that sooner or later you'd be around.'

'But how?'

'Don't you try to tell me, Commissario,' she said pointing the Tuscan cigar at him, 'that you don't know perfectly well about his visits here.'

Peroni decided it wasn't worth denying this. 'Quite true,' he said, noticing with surprise that he had instinctively dropped into the role of admiring literary critic, 'I knew about the visits, but not about the reason for them.'

'And you think his death may have something to do with that?'

The admiring literary critic had a job not to look taken aback. 'I can't very well say that,' he said judiciously, 'until I know what the reason was.'

'Too true,' she said, smiling with big yellow teeth as though he had expressed a particularly deft judgement, 'Alice! Hurry up with that whisky! Well, I won't attempt to hold anything back,'

61

she continued to Peroni, 'I've got too much experience of you policemen to try and do anything as silly as that. He came to see me about – Ah, Alice, here you are at last. Put it down there. Now then, Commissario, don't bother to say when – we'll have two stiff ones. Help yourself to water. Chin chin, Commissario!'

'Chin chin,' said the admiring literary critic.

'Where were we then? Yes, that's right. Young Florio-Levi came to see me about my new book.'

'A crime novel?' enquired Peroni, feeling he might have stumbled on something solid at last.

'No, no,' she said, disappointing him, 'I don't confine myself to crime fiction, Commissario. I turn my hand to anything that's going. I'm a literary jack-of-all-trades and, mark my words, it's the only way to be a real professional. People who only work in one genre are nothing but piffling amateurs! No, no – novels, criticism, biography, history, drama – even poetry, God forgive me – they're all grist to my mill.'

'And what was this particular book?'

'Is, Commissario, not was – it's still in the workshop. It's a biography.'

'A biography of whom?' Peroni enunciated carefully, a prickling feeling running down his neck.

'A woman called Jacopa de Settesoli,' said Dame Iolanthe Higgins, 'I don't know if you've heard of her.'

'As a matter of fact, I have. I saw her tomb yesterday. Did Florio-Levi say why he was interested in her?'

'Something about a thesis, wasn't it, Alice?'

'Yes, dear.'

'Did he happen to mention how he got to know about you?'

'Iolanthe's very famous,' Alice rallied quaveringly to her friend.

'Don't start talking a lot of rot, Alice.' The Dame pulled thoughtfully at her Tuscan cigar. 'You've got a point there, Commissario,' she said after a second. 'Didn't give any thought to it at the time. Agreeable enough young man turns up on the doorstep – how d'you do – how d'you do – believe you're writing a life of Jacopa de Settesoli – Absolutely right – I'm interested in her for a thesis about medieval Assisi – you'd better come along in and have a glass of something. Those were the general lines on which the dialogue ran, weren't they Alice?'

'Does number 12 Via Pozzo della Mensa mean anything to you?'

'Good heavens, yes! That's the house where Jacopa probably lived after the death of Francis.'

'It was Iolanthe who discovered the connection,' said Alice proudly.

This time Dame Iolanthe did not shout her friend down; instead she took a swallow of whisky and allowed a glow of satisfaction to suffuse her stern masculine features. 'True enough,' she said, 'I was, in fact, lucky enough to trace certain documents which indicate that Jacopa spent the last years of her life in that house.'

'So you must have visited it?'

'At one time I was in and out of it practically every day. That was about a year ago when I first got onto it. The house was lived in by a poor old biddy at the time, all alone in the world and partly paralysed as well. Then she died and I haven't been back since. I understand the place is lived in by some sort of high-class trollop now.' A thought struck her. 'You don't mean to say that young Florio-Levi went there, too?' Peroni nodded. 'Well, well, well!' she said reflectively and then suddenly heaved with an unexpectedly bawdy giggle. 'Daresay there was a certain amount of slap and tickle with the trollop, eh? From all one hears, Florio-Levi was a bit of a young goat.' The bawdiness passed as quickly as it had come, and she was once again the literary panjandrum. 'Yes, well, that's quite enough of that,' she told herself sternly.

'How many times did Lorenzo visit you?' Peroni asked.

'About four times, wasn't it, Alice?'

'Three, dear. The first time —'

'Yes, well, we won't niggle about that. Three or four.'

'And each time the talk was of Jacopa de Settesoli?'

'That's right. Oh, I daresay we passed the time of day about the weather and so on, but the burden was always Jacopa.' She paused, then leant forward portentously on a pile of books. 'Do you suppose *now*, Commissario, that she can have had something to do with Lorenzo being killed?'

'Before answering that, it looks as though I shall have to learn something more about her myself. I know very little. Perhaps you would be prepared to teach me?'

'You've touched my weak point there, Commissario. Let's have another glass of whisky.'

'But Iolanthe —'

'Shut up, Alice!' She refilled the two glasses, then leaned magisterially back in her chair. 'Let us start with the little that was known of her until I was lucky enough last year – I use the word advisedly, for it was a sheer case of serendipity – to discover certain material concerning her which had been overlooked for seven centuries. She was born in about 1190 with a heady mixture of Norman and Sicilian blood. When she was nineteen she married a Roman nobleman. Her eldest son was born approximately a year after the marriage, and two years after that she met Francis for the first time. A deep and mysterious friendship was established between them, and he was always a welcome guest at her Roman home. We know that she made him almond cream cakes, a delicacy of which he was particularly fond – an interesting detail, this, for it's the only recorded case of Francis indulging, even as innocently as that, in the pleasures of the palate.'

Dame Iolanthe interrupted briefly to indulge her own palate with whisky and a long draw at the Tuscan cigar, then she continued.

'He gave her a lamb which he had rescued from the slaughter, and it became so fond of her that it used to follow her to Mass in the morning – wouldn't be able to do that nowadays with all that damn traffic – and wake her with gentle little buttings of its head if she was late in getting up.

'Both the lamb and the almond cakes are involved in her last meeting with Francis. In 1226 she felt a sudden irresistible impulsion to go and see Francis in Assisi. She hastily made some almond cakes and then, taking a robe she had spun for him with the wool of the lamb, she left for Assisi. When she arrived, she learned that he was dying and was on the point of dictating a letter to her asking her to come. So she was able to salute him for the last time, and when his eyes finally closed for ever a few days later, she was the first person admitted to see his body.

'About nine years previously, shortly after the birth of her second son, her husband had died, so there was nothing now, she realised, to prevent her spending the rest of her life in Assisi. And this she did, dying some time towards the end of the thirteenth century.'

These last words were followed by a brief silence, interrupted by what sounded like a low rumble of thunder which did not, however, come from outside. Its place of origin was Dame Iolanthe's stomach, and its authoress, quite unembarrassed, confirmed this.

'That,' she announced, 'is my inner man. The poor fellow must be starved to death. Why don't you stay and have a bite to eat, Commissario, and I'll tell you over table about my extraordinary find?'

'I wouldn't like to disturb —'

'No disturbance at all! We're delighted to have you, aren't we, Alice?'

'Of *course* we are,' said Alice, timidly, but apparently sincerely. 'The food's in the oven and it won't take me a second to lay a third place.'

Saying this she fluttered out of the room while the Dame, wheezing with bronchial protest at the Tuscan cigar, extracted her trousered lower limbs from the heaving sea of cats and books. 'I'll say this for Alice,' she said as she did so, 'she's a damn fine cook. Simple but good. She'll give you the best shepherd's pie you've ever tasted.'

'Shepherd's pie?' said Peroni, whose fervent anglophilia had somehow overlooked this. She explained with a wealth of references, literary, historical, geographical and humorous ('First take one well covered shepherd. . . .') at the same time leading him into the dining room.

This room must have been small to start with when bare of furniture, but crowded as it was with a polished dining-room table and chairs, a sideboard and three glass-fronted cabinets filled with china collector's pieces, and lit only by candlelight, which caused the shadows to press silently in, it seemed about as ample as a medium-sized bird-cage.

'Afraid it's a bit of a squash, Commissario,' said Dame Iolanthe, 'but you'll find it perfectly comfortable once you're in. We've had dinner parties for twelve in our time, haven't we Alice? Now see what you think of this shepherd's pie, Commissario – just as it ought to be: golden brown on top, near white just below the surface and sizzling and bubbling like hell deep down inside. Let me pour you a glass of wine, Commissario – it's a Trebbiano, which is about the best we can get round here. Yes, well, I daresay you're anxious to hear the next episode of the story.'

Peroni said that he was indeed and the Dame, having champed a couple of pensive mouthfuls of shepherd's pie and transfixed Alice with a brief but masterful glare, embarked once again on her narrative.

Undignified Pursuit of Petrarch

'It all began one foggy winter day rather over a year ago,' began Dame Iolanthe in fine story-telling fettle. 'We were in Rome at the time staying with friends, and they drew my attention to an auction being held that afternoon at the home of a certain noble family known as the Frangipani. Seems that only one member of the family was still surviving, an elderly gentleman, and that he had decided to shut up most of the palace, and install himself and his own few belongings in a small flat at the top of the building.'

'Well, as I daresay you've noticed – nothing escapes a policeman's eye – I'm a bit of a collector myself and I never miss the chance to pick up something good, so along I toddled all on my own, didn't I Alice?'

'Yes, dear, I had a dreadful headache.'

'As I said, it was foggy that day. Rome's an odd sort of place at the best of times – the catacombs and the ruins of the imperial city sticking up against the sky like the broken teeth of a prehistoric monster —' Really getting into her literary stride, thought Peroni, who was enjoying himself. '— Not to mention that dreadful church in the Via Veneto with its four thousand skeletons. The list could go on indefinitely. But when it's foggy, well, the past is like a skilful private eye shadowing you wherever you go, and always managing to keep just out of sight if you turn round to catch him. And fog or no fog, the Frangipani palace is a strange enough sort of place in its own right.' Huge, crumbling, dusty, full of echoes – and cold, too. You could safely have stored frozen beef there.

'It wasn't too bad in the hall where the auction was being held. They'd got some sort of rudimentary heating in there – a bit like Geppetto's candle in the tummy of the giant fish, but better than nothing – and there was a certain amount of noise and movement. Trouble was, though, they were selling a lot of stuff that didn't interest me – massive pieces of furniture. I enquired about the stuff I was after, and they said it was coming up in about an hour, so I went off for a wander round the house by myself. Most of it was already closed up, but I found one large room still open, and that turned out to be a library.

'Well, when I get loose in a library there's no holding me, and this was a very interesting library, too. I knew the books were eventually going to be auctioned, too, so I thought it would do no harm to have a private preview, and I started to look around. Fair amount of rubbish, but a lot of fascinating stuff, too. Then on a top shelf I spotted what looked like a very old edition of Petrarch's *Canzoniere*. If it was good and as old as I thought, then it would be well worth bidding for, but I had to look at the thing. Now this was easier said than done. There was a ladder, but it was as ancient as everything else and looked exceedingly frail, and I'm not exactly what you might call a nymph, am I Alice? Still, beggars can't be choosers, and I wasn't going to let that *Canzoniere* slip through my fingers without a struggle, so I propped the ladder in the appropriate position and started to climb up. I was almost at the top and the *Canzoniere* was within my grasp when something gave. I clutched at the nearest thing to hand, which was a shelf, and hung on for all I was worth.'

Peroni could just see the Dame in this dangerous predicament, and the spectacle was such that he had to take a careful swallow of Trebbiano in order to keep a straight face.

67

'Unfortunately – or fortunately as it turned out – this shelf wasn't any too firm either. It didn't actually give way, but it cracked, displacing a number of books, some of which fell about my head. Well, by the time I'd succeeded in climbing down more or less in one piece, the thought that was uppermost in my mind was no longer the *Canzoniere*, but the damage I'd done. I picked up the books that had fallen and tried to arrange them more or less tidily, and while I was doing so I noticed that one of them wasn't a book at all, but a sort of leather wallet. Very ancient. Curiosity got the better of me and I opened it. There were some sheets inside, probably as old as the wallet; couldn't put a date to them, of course, but they were certainly older than the Petrarch. Remarkably well preserved, too, which must have been something to do with the leather of the wallet. They were covered with rapid, very attractive handwriting. I'm no graphologist, but there's some handwriting which makes you think – there's a good mind and a good heart behind that. Well, that's how it was with this handwriting. The stuff was in Italian, but an Italian long before Manzoni got his hands onto it. If the light had been better, I could have made out a bit and with expert help a lot, but as things were I could decipher nothing of the sense. And yet – I don't know if you know how it is, Commissario, there are moments in life when you feel that you're onto something very big indeed.'

'Yes, I do know,' said Peroni, who was something of a specialist in such moments.

'There's a sensible man,' said the Dame approvingly. 'Well, this was one of those moments. But I was in a bit of a predicament. Almost certainly nobody knew of its existence, but I could hardly just pinch it, could I? Then after some quick, hard thinking I reached what you might consider a somewhat Jesuitical compromise. I decided to borrow it. Later, when I had found out exactly what it was, I would restore it and make a clean breast of the whole thing. Fortunately, I always carry about with me a somewhat voluminous shopping bag just in case I should come across anything interesting. Though normally, of course,' the Dame added hastily, 'I pay.'

'Of course,' said Peroni.

'I immediately put this project into effect. All thoughts of the

Canzoniere having vanished from my mind, I popped the wallet into my bag and made my way out. Then, with the help of an expert, I translated the contents of the pages into modern Italian. The result, Commissario, left me gaping, dumbfounded. Ah, good, Alice – the pudding. Alice's apple pie is a fitting companion for her shepherd's ditto. Where was I? Yes, dumbfounded. The material consisted of three letters, or rather extracts from three letters, for pages were obviously missing. One had the impression that somebody, at a date subsequent to the writing of the letters, had decided to collect them together, only to discover that bits had been lost or thrown away, but this does nothing to detract from their extraordinary freshness, elegance of style, humour and, at moments, startling profundity.

'The writer is evidently a young woman, and the recipients are her two sons, Giovanni and Graziano. The only date mentioned throughout the extracts is May 1230 (one has the impression that the young woman was not overly precise about her dates anyway) and it's clear that they were all written prior to that date. There are no addresses, of course, but it seems probable that the two boys were in Rome, while it is unquestionable that the young woman was in Assisi. And Assisi, moreover, at an exceedingly significant moment of its history. St Francis had died about two years previously, and been canonised just before the writing of the first letter. The city was in a state of tumultuous ferment. Pilgrims were pouring in from all over Europe and the citizens were doing their pitifully inadequate best to provide food and accommodation for them and, of course at the same time, to exploit the seemingly inexhaustible gold-mine which the situation had become.

'And as if all this wasn't enough, the city also had to cope with the enormous work force engaged on building the basilica, the greatest in Christendom at that time. It is hard to imagine the explosion of labour this involved. Many cathedrals took centuries to build, and fifty years was a mere eyelid's blink in such construction, but here the entire lower church was finished in 1230, a mere two years after work had started. The nearest parallel to such an undertaking nowadays is the construction of something like the Mont Blanc tunnel with all the attendant danger and tension.

'So the Assisi in which this young woman was living, far from being the peaceful retreat at the green heart of Umbria as sentimental idiots try to portray it, was a centre of febrile activity, crammed to way beyond bursting point with craftsmen, artisans, masons, artists, sculptors, friars, pilgrims, tourists and a fair sprinkling of vagabonds, pick-pockets and other miscellaneous riff-raff.

'One other thing is immediately evident: she had known Francis personally. The relationship is almost entirely implicit in the letters, and there are none of the facts one would like to know – how she met him and when, what they said and so on. But it is obvious that, whatever the factual data, the relationship must have been a particularly intense one. Our perspectives are so warped by Eros that it's hard for us to conceive that a man like Dante, for example, could have had his entire life changed by a girl he had scarcely more than seen, and at the same time find in her the inspiration and driving force for one of the greatest masterpieces in the history of the world. But something not unlike that must have happened here.

'Unfortunately for the young woman in question, this relationship of hers with Francis was beginning to be public knowledge at the time of the letters, and she was being increasingly pestered and besieged by the faithful, but also by the curious. She can be funny and often biting about this, and it's not hard to gather that she's in a fair state of exasperation.

'Well, there I was with this fascinating material and not even the slightest idea how to handle it because, however fascinating from a human and literary point of view, it was too incomplete to publish by itself. The only thing would be to trace the identity of the writer, but that seemed impossible after seven centuries. Then I had the sense to do what I should have done immediately – read a life of Francis.

'I realised at once that Jacopa de Settesoli – that apparently "minor" character – fitted the description perfectly. But that was a long way from proving the case. So I went into it a bit more deeply, and this time I came back with a real plum – or more exactly two plums. Jacopa had two sons named Giovanni and Graziano. As far as I was concerned that clinched it, but I was going to need more than that to convince the experts. And by thunder, Commissario, I got it! I discovered that the name de Settesoli was only a form of nickname, derived from the Septizonium castle which the family owned on the Esquiline hill –a name which still survives today in the Roman Via dei Sette Soli. The real family name was Frangipani. Wonder of wonders! For it was in the Frangipani library in Rome that I had, by sheer serendipity, discovered the letters in the first place. And that, Commissario, is both the end of that particular story and the beginning of my book.'

When Dame Iolanthe came to an end, admiring silence hung on the air almost as perceptibly as the smell of Alice's cooking. Peroni, the respectful literary critic, let her enjoy it, feeling that she had after all earned it. Then finally he said, 'A most remarkable story.'

'Iolanthe is a remarkable woman,' said Alice.

'Don't start talking tosh, Alice!'

'And this is the story you told Lorenzo?'

'Word for word.'

'Did he read the letters?'

'Yes, I let him see a copy.'

'Perhaps you would let me read them, too?'

'By all means. Tell you what, there's a quiz programme on the telly now which I never miss if I can help it – amazing how some people's minds work, retaining all that stuff when it's all I can do to remember my own name – anyway, you settle yourself comfortably in here and Alice'll bring you a cup of Irish coffee with the letters in translation and a Xerox copy of the original. Then when we've both finished, we can meet up again for some more Irish coffee and a talk. How would that be?'

'That,' said Peroni with the air of a literary critic approving a masterpiece, 'would be absolutely fine.'

The Eye Claims its Share

'. . . . now that the canonisation is over, Assisi is less crowded – instead of sleeping twenty-five to a bed, they're now only sleeping twenty.'

The opening of the first letter was missing and this was the existing start which Peroni now read. First he had examined the Xerox copies of the original and found himself concurring unreservedly with Dame Iolanthe's judgement that behind this handwriting there was a good mind and a good heart. Intellectually this gave satisfaction, but as an Italian proverb puts it 'The eye claims its share,' and he fervently wished that he could form some idea of what Jacopa had looked like in the living flesh. For a second he dreamed impotently, then went on with his reading.

'It's like living in the middle of a continual fair – you two would simply love it. Come to that, I don't mind it myself. I enjoy the noise and bustle and variety, and nothing could be more delightful than the sideshows which spring up spontaneously at every street corner like mushrooms after rain: fire-eaters, dancers, tumblers, singers, players on pipes and tabors and lutes and every conceivable instrument. No, I certainly don't complain about all this, for there is worse than cheerful uproar to try me.

'More and more people are coming to learn of the friendship between Francis and me, and they seek me out expecting to find a saint! Could anything be more absurd? Your poor, fallible, short-tempered, dagger-tongued mother! I have an abundant foretaste of the torments of purgatory when I force myself into the hair shirt of this pious stranger they are expecting to meet. Why do it then? I can hear you both asking. Why indeed? For one thing. when I am treated as a relic a most terrible spell is cast upon me so that I become quite incapable of behaving naturally. For another, I have the feeling that I would be injuring Francis – though God knows he is far beyond all injury now! – if I were to let these trusting pilgrims see my true, disgraceful self; instead of crowding to Assisi, as is certainly for the good of their souls, they would flee from it in horror.

'I could give you many instances of this well-meaning, muddle-headed attitude which insists on seeing me as a sort of cross between leviathan and St Simeon Stylites on his pillar, but I will limit myself to one. I was invited to supper the other day by messer Ugo da Palazzo, the Captain of the People of Assisi, a man much noted for his avidity. Of course, being me, I couldn't help reflecting that I've lived here for two years without receiving

72

such an invitation. Could it just be that Francis's canonisation has made me officially respectable? However, I went.

'My entrance, like an acorn with the potentiality of an oak, contained in miniature the entire awful evening. As you both very well know, I have always tried to dress simply but well. This was my rule before I met Francis and it remains so now that he is dead. The only outward concession that I make to his memory is that I always have a tau cross sewn upon my cloak. But on my arrival in the hall that evening I saw from the expressions of the company that they were expecting some sort of outlandish scarecrow with straws sticking out of its hair. The women looked outraged, but the reaction of the men was even worse. They obviously thought that contact with Francis had the effect of automatically and overnight depriving a woman of all traces of femininity, so when they discovered that I was at least as much a creature of flesh and blood as they were, the results were very unpleasant to behold. Their eyes bulged, their mouths dropped open, their faces grew red, and the sound of their breathing was louder than the panting of the hounds.

'The worst of them all was my host, messer Ugo. He is a small man, but he more than makes up for this in girth. His little red eyes put you in mind of a boar facing its hunters, and indeed his general behaviour has much in common with that of the same animal. The remarkable effect my appearance had upon him alarmed me considerably until I perceived with relief that his wife was no less aware of it and intended to take matters in hand. This she did by insisting that we go to table, where she placed me safely between herself and another good wife of the household.

'My relief, however, was short lived for dame Emilia and the other excellent lady began to harass me exceedingly about the miracles of Francis, or what they were pleased to consider his miracles. Had I ever seen a miracle? (Their disappointment when I said no seemed to shut them up for a good half second.) Was it true that he could walk on water? Had I seen the marks of the stigmata? It seemed as though they had agreed upon their plan of attack beforehand, for although both of them ate and drank prodigiously, they never left me unquestioned, but took it in turns to consume and enquire, so while on one hand there was champing and slurping, on the other there was yet another interrogative about Francis's magic powers. I thought they would never run out, and could find no better consolation for myself than to think that at least matters could not get worse.

'But they could. When dame Emilia and her companion had reluctantly satisfied themselves that the well of my memory was dry of magic secrets, they started off on a yet more deplorable quest. Did I have any relics? Scraps of his habit, locks of his hair, shavings from his beard, parings of his nails – anything. These things, they told me, were in much demand as love potions and talismans for warding off the evil eye or amassing large quantities of money. In view of this, added dame Emilia (and I perceived now the true motive for which I had been invited) they were prepared to pay good sums for any such articles, so long as I would guarantee their genuineness with my authenticated mark – I fear that, not being able to write themselves, they took it for granted that I could not do so either.

'How could I tell them that the only relic of Francis I have or wish to have is a burning coal of love in my heart which is never extinguished by day or night?

'I cast desperately about me for a way of escape, but there seemed to be none: the wall was behind me, the ladies on either side and the table before.

'And then I happened to catch some snatches of the men's conversation. They were talking about the crusades and were divided about the outcome. This division depended upon their opinion of the Emperor Frederick. Some held that he would win Jerusalem by force of arms, others said that his army – already sadly depleted by the epidemic of plague which broke out during the previous abortive visit to the Holy Land – could never stand before the Arabs and would soon be routed. This difference, inflamed by massive quantities of wine, promised dangerously for an intruder, but I had little alternative.

' "Frederick's army will neither conquer Jerusalem," I said, "nor be routed."

'The good ladies who had been so fervently seeking miracles should have been content, for those few words threw the whole table into the most absolute silence. They all looked at me as though I had been stricken with sudden leprosy, and through the silence you could hear the crackling of the fire. It was messer Ugo who eventually decided to intervene.

'"How can you, a wo—" (He had been about to say 'a woman', but he interrupted his boar's snarl just in time.) "How can you pretend to foresee such matters?"

'"I *foresee* nothing," I said hastily, stamping on another miracle before it was hatched. "I know the Emperor and the circumstances so it is quite possible to calculate what will happen."

'"You *know* the Emperor?" Brother Boar – as Francis would have called him – looked as though his hunters had unexpectedly thrown away their spears.

'"When he was fourteen and his mother died," I said, "he was made a ward of the Pope, which meant that he spent a lot of his time in Rome where my family lived. He was frequently our guest, and as we are much of an age and both of Norman blood we became close friends and have remained so ever since. Until I came to Assisi, he would always visit us in Rome when he was there."

'At this messer Ugo halted in the very act of charging, but one of his companions broke cover and came to his aid. "Can you describe the Emperor?" he asked, and you could tell that this one must at least have seen Frederick, even if only from a distance, and thought to give me the lie with facts.

'"He is of medium height," I said, "but well-built, sturdy and athletic looking. You can see clearly in his features the mixture of German and Norman blood he inherited from his parents. He is somewhat dark complexioned, though his cheeks are surprisingly pink. His eyes are a light blue and they squint almost imperceptibly. He has a prominent nose, a forceful chin and somewhat thin, nervous lips. The expression you can most clearly read on his features is one of irony."

'This description caused the second man to sneak back growling where he had come from but messer Ugo was now ready to attack again.

'"Even if you do know the Emperor," he said, "you can't possibly tell how his fortunes in or out of battle will go."

' "I don't pretend to tell or foretell any such fortunes," I replied, "but we have often talked together of such things, and I know how he thinks."

'Dame Emilia and the rest of the women were goggling at me as though I had suddenly sprouted a unicorn's horn; I don't think they had ever heard a woman discussing such things with men before. But as you both know it was a tradition in my father's household that women should be treated as reasonable creatures; the same tradition passed into our family when your father was alive, and it did not die with him.

' "But what you say is a manifold absurdity," said Brother Boar, now spluttering, "You said that Frederick's army will neither conquer Jerusalem nor be routed. That is impossible! One of the two alternatives must inevitably occur."

' "No," I said, "for there is a third possibility. Agreement can be reached through diplomatic channels."

' "Diplomatic channels! With the Arabs?"

'At this he started to laugh, and the rest of the table dutifully followed him. I waited, knowing that I could afford to, and indeed after some seconds their laughter began to recede as they perceived that my store of knowledge was not exhausted. Only when the silence was once again absolute and their curiosity had reached boiling point, did I start to speak again. "Two days ago," I said, "I received a report from my cousin who is with the Emperor. He told me how the Christian troops who were already there refused to fight with Frederick and how he, as a result, decided to reach an agreement with the Sultan Al Kamil. Embassies of great cordiality were exchanged and the two shortly became firm friends. The Sultan, said my cousin, was deeply impressed by the Emperor's exhaustive knowledge of Arab culture and a treaty is already being discussed. It is expected that the Sultan will concede to the Emperor not only Jerusalem, but also Acri, Jaffa, Sidon, Nazareth and Bethlehem. Without a drop of blood being shed."

'I do not expect to be invited to the Captain of the People's table again and, curiously enough, have few regrets about this.

'I hope the two of you are behaving with a civilised minimum of decorum and that you, Graziano, are correcting your vision of

76

the world as a private orchard in which all the juiciest apples belong to you. As for you, Giovanni, I look forward to hearing that you are acquiring some elements of self restraint. I do not condemn your tendency to throw yourself headlong into adventure without regard for the consequences, for it is a trait that goes hand in hand with courage and generosity, but like a high mettled horse, it needs firm control.

'When next you hear of travellers on the road for Assisi, send me a letter by means of them. I purpose to visit Rome in the spring. I embrace you both.

'Your neglectful, unworthy but always loving
   Mother.'

In one gulp, Peroni finished his Irish coffee, which had got almost completely cold as he read. His eye now was not claiming, but clamouring for its share. She must have been an attractive woman to have aroused such emotions at messer Ugo's table, but what type? Full-lipped and fleshy with nectar-tender eyes? No, way off target. Too much humour and common-sense about her. A more northern type then? Straight, classical features, firmly-set lips, sensible eyes? No, that was just as bad. She was too undilutedly feminine and impulsive. Peroni guessed that Giovanni had inherited from her his tendency to throw himself headlong into adventure.

Peroni searched the smoke of an English black market cigarette, but her face was not there. He started to read again.

Cherished Giovanni and Graziano,
   I cannot describe to you the joy with which I received your letter when the Contessa Angela arrived here the other day on her way to Paris. Her visit was the occasion of an incident which, although it has its funny side, was anything but funny at the time.

'As you know, all those who pass through Assisi are afire to see the mighty edifice which is going up in memory of Francis, two great churches, one on top of the other, forming a single mighty basilica, the greatest wonder of the world, the supreme achievement of human hands and so on and so on. Personally,

I'm in two minds about the whole thing. Oh, I know all the arguments in favour of it: nothing smaller would accommodate the countless pilgrims who will flock to Assisi throughout the ages to come, and nothing less would do sufficient honour to the sanctity of Francis. But there are moments when I can't help wondering whether it's not just a little in bad taste. Oh, I don't mean artistically or archeologically, of course, but Francis considered himself essentially a "little" man, and I wonder if it's right that a "little" man should have such a very big edifice to be buried in. Moses was buried in a valley where no man might ever know of his sepulchre. I'm sure that's what Francis would have preferred, too.

'Anyway, whether we like it or not, we've got it and, as I said, everybody who comes to Assisi wants to see it. Angela was no exception. But there is a snag about this. Brother Elias who is building it – I'll come to him in a minute – is insistent that the whole thing should be wrapped in mystery till the last minute. There are fences almost as ambitious as the building itself, guards, keys and passwords. And now that efforts are being doubled, re-doubled and doubled again to finish the lower of the two churches by spring next year when Francis's body will be transferred from the church of San Giorgio where it now lies to the vault here where it will for ever lie, the secrecy and precautions have been magnified in proportion to these efforts.

'But Angela was insistent and, as you know, one might as well reason with a battering ram as with Angela's insistence.

'Well, I made enquiries – or, if you prefer, set spies to work – and I discovered that at ten o'clock the following morning Brother Elias would be at a chapter meeting, and with him out of the way it all became much easier. I know most of the people involved, guards included, and I was sure they would let us slip in for a few minutes so long as he never got to know about it.

'I daresay you will be asking, "Who is this Brother Elias that so tyrannises over everybody?" The simple answer is that, having acted as a sort of human hair-shirt for Francis during his lifetime, he is now doing his best to continue this function after Francis's death. He is a man of great zeal, inexhaustible energy, sheer ruthlessness and most unlovable nature. And the strangest paradox of all is that he is exactly the man whom God, in His inscrutability, wanted first of all at Francis's side and now at the Head of his Order. Francis recognised this and always treated him with the greatest love and deference.

'Brother Elias is carrying forward his unimaginably colossal project for the basilica with an apparently super-human driving power that is no less astonishing than the edifice itself.

'One more thing I should add about him is that he has seen through me. He knows all my faults, weaknesses and vanities, and rightly considers it a scandal that a woman such as me (perhaps any woman, come to that) should be linked with the man to whose glory he is dedicating his extraordinary forces and talents. Consequently the very sight of me is anathema to him, and he would do anything in his power to get me out of Assisi.

'Anyway, shortly after ten o'clock the following morning, with this man safely engaged in his chapter meeting, Angela and I moved in on the unfinished basilica, and as I'd foreseen we had no trouble getting in.

'The spectacle is impressive. The building gives the impression of an enormous underground fortification built to withstand the most savage onslaught. The vaulting is of extraordinary power; if stone had muscles, you feel, this is how they would look. The strength of the place is emphasised by the fact that it is totally unadorned so that you feel physically crushed by the sheer mass of stone. This will soon be painted over, and the place will be alive with colour, but I think that nothing will ever equal the austerity of its nakedness.

'We went down the steps to the crypt where Francis's body will lie, and here the impression of being at the heart of a kingdom of stone becomes almost unbearable. It was as we were emerging, with some relief, from the crypt that we were transfixed by the most terrible howl of rage.

' "Who are those women?"

'It was Brother Elias. (I later discovered that the chapter meeting had been postponed at the last minute, but at the time I was too alarmed to reason: he was simply *there*.) At this cry of his, the building was transformed into a wild flutter of activity as when feeding pigeons are suddenly alarmed. Brothers and masons ran agitatedly here and there as though they were looking for a fire, and at the same time Brother Elias bore down upon us like a storm cloud in human form.

'When he recognised that one of the two sacrilegious intruders was me, his anger become completely pure. He threatened us with ,excommunication, he said he would have us arraigned before the Pope, he demanded that we be thrust incontinently into outer darkness.

'There was much I could have said, but it was easier just to go.

'When I had returned home and was beginning to recover from the sheer violence of it, the sense of humiliation began to set in, and that was far worse. Francis said we should accept humiliation cheerfully as the most infallible medicine for the ills of our soul, but personally I could more cheerfully have put up with leprosy.

'That evening, however, after poor Angela had left, still not very clear in her mind about what had happened, I had a visit of much consolation.

'Do you remember, Graziano, how I took you one day to a little hermitage on Monte Ripido near Perugia where there was a friar called Brother Giles living alone? He took two sticks and played as if on the violin, scraping one across the other, and talking at the same time so sublimely of the love of God that not only was it not ridiculous, but that it almost seemed as though you could hear the music?

'Well, that evening Brother Giles called to see me, and the very instant he entered the sense of boiling outrage that was consuming me vanished, leaving behind a cool, sweet sense of contentment.

' "So that's better then," he said smiling.

'Then he looked serious. "Unfortunately, not everything is so easily put to rights," he said, and suddenly his face was contracted with such pain that I thought he must be ill.

' "What's the matter?" I cried.

' "Blood," he said, "I see blood." '

An Eagle from Venice

So deeply had Peroni become involved with Jacopa's account that it took him an instant to scramble back up the centuries when a tap came at the door. '*Avanti*,' he called.

'Iolanthe,' said Alice, popping her head in, 'thought you would like another Irish coffee.'

'That's very kind of her.'

'They're just starting the double or nothing bit. There's a man who knows simply everything about mountaineering, and Iolanthe's very keen to see whether he doubles or not, but after that she'll be free.'

Peroni looked at the pages still remaining. 'I shouldn't be very long either,' he said.

'I won't disturb you any more then,' said Alice, and depositing the cup before him, tip-toed with mouse-like reverence out of the room.

Blood, thought Peroni, sipping the heavily-laced coffee, whatever could Brother Giles have meant by that? Unfortunately, the document was no help for, after Jacopa had put much the same question herself, the page came to an end, and the following one was missing.

Could Brother Giles conceivably have foreseen something specific? One thing was sure. The future for them, that evening in Assisi, was the past for Peroni, so that if something had been going to happen, it had now happened. Could that something have a bearing on the death of Lorenzo Florio-Levi?

These thoughts pattered like mice on one level of Peroni's ramshackle mind. At another level, lower down, the smoke continued to swirl, forming trial portraits of Jacopa. But as soon as the swirling began to resemble something like a face it had to be dissipated because, attractive though it might be, it was not Jacopa's.

He picked up the third letter.

*

'. . . . adventures of all sorts. Usually mothers don't tell their sons of such things, but I have always tried to be open with you, and besides I want your ratification for the decision I have made. Or hope I have made, for women can be dangerously inconstant. Let me start at the beginning.

'You're probably too young – even you, Giovanni – to realise how often the weather takes a hand in one's life. On this occasion, after some days of rain, I woke up to the sort of day I believe you can find nowhere on earth but in Assisi. I got ready quickly and went out to do some shopping at the stalls in the square.

'It was while I was examining the vegetables with the air of a shrewd housewife which I pretend intimidates the stall-holders that I became aware of a man observing me. I couldn't see him, but I was as aware of male eyes upon me as I would have been of a trumpet blast. Of course I gave no sign of my awareness and concentrated my attention more closely on the vegetables, hoping the eyes would go away. But they didn't. I could feel them unwavering on my back. What could a poor widow do? Escape was impossible, for I was obliged to pass that way. I decided to turn about slowly and quell the eyes with a dreadful and imperious look.

'But I had scarcely started to put this plan into effect when it was shattered by the sight of the eyes' owner. He was a great lord of the sort to which I am no longer accustomed, having purposed to abandon the glories of this world. He was wearing a red mantle bordered with gold over a white tunic, and the sheath of his sword was sewn with precious stones. But the splendour of his raiment was nothing to that of his face and figure. And as if that weren't enough, I had the impression I had seen him somewhere before.

' "Jacopa!"

'As he called my name, the years fell away like a cloak. Michele Aquila. His place in my life was long before you, and indeed before your father, for we were children together. Aquila – I always called him that because he soared like an eagle – was as brilliant as he was beautiful, and at twelve he was already deeply versed in philosophy, theology, history, astronomy, music and botany as well as being able to speak seven languages, including

Greek and Hebrew.

'The stallholder must have been dumbfounded at the sight of a modest widow being swept into the embrace of such a great lord, and indeed doing her own part in the sweeping amid a wild scattering of vegetables.

'"Aquila!"

'"So you remember me?"

'"Is that so surprising? You remembered me first – and from my back, too."

'"The memory of you is more clear in my mind than that of anyone I have ever met since. You haven't changed, Jacopa."

'His tone as he said this was altogether too serious to be safe, and I thought it best to bring him down to earth. "That can hardly be," I said, "seeing that I am the mother of two sons, and one of them already grown."

'"You're married then?" Female vanity made me think that he looked downcast.

'"I am a widow." That same vanity made me imagine renewed hope flaming in his features like a beacon.

'"The word 'widow' ill becomes you; it is like describing a rose as a plant – accurate enough as far as it goes, but quite missing the beauty of the truth."

'I could see that things were likely to get out of control altogether if I did not take some decisive action. "It is good to meet you again, Aquila," I said, "but we must remember our stations. You are evidently a great lord with great matters to attend to. I, more modestly, have the shopping."

'"No matter could be of more consequence than you, Jacopa. And as for the shopping, it won't be necessary, as you will dine with me."

'Did I do wrong? I let him have his way. Within a few minutes, it seemed, he had got hold of two magnificently caparisoned horses, and we were riding together out of Assisi towards Santa Maria degli Angeli.

'"You ride as perfectly as ever," he said. This was a compliment I appreciated for I ride little these days and am more accustomed to mules than to magnificent horses such as that.

'"What brings you to Assisi?" I asked him.

' "Matters of state. I am accompanying His Excellency Bartolomeo Morosino, the Venetian ambassador, who is paying a visit of state to your Captain of the People."

' "How exciting."

' "I assure you it's not – state visits are the dullest things in the world. And you, Jacopa, what brings you to Assisi?"

'I told him of my friendship with Francis and how, on his death, I had preferred to come and live in Assisi rather than stay on in Rome.

' "Surely Venice would be a more golden choice than either?"

'I started to gallop on ahead of him; it seemed simpler than finding an answer.

'Shortly after this we stopped, and Aquila unloaded a veritable banquet from his horse: quails and swan and venison, with half a dozen cheeses and newly baked bread and an abundance of wine.

' "You remember?"

'I didn't have to ask what he was referring to. When we were children, we used to collect food from the pantries of our homes and ride into the country outside Rome where he would course with his hawk and we would both run until we were exhausted and then collapse on the grass and eat our meal. "I remember," I said.

' "And here we are back again as though nothing had happened in between."

' "But things have happened."

' "They can be forgotten."

' "A husband and two children? And what about you? There must have been many – events in your life."

' "None that didn't dwindle into non-existence when I saw you examining the vegetables as though you were trying them for some heinous crime. I've grown up since we last met, Jacopa, and I've become what you're pleased to call a great lord. But inside me the irreverent little boy who used to ride out hawking with you is still very much alive."

'This I already knew. I had seen him. I had recognised him.

' "He loved you then, and he still loves you now."

'And maybe I loved him, too. But I didn't dare say anything for fear that what little resolve I had would collapse altogether.

' "Come to Venice, Jacopa. It's the most exciting city in the world. It could offer your two boys brilliant careers, and nothing would please me better than to be a father to them."

'This was the deadliest temptation of all, and I think I might have fallen to it if I hadn't looked up at the huddle of buildings that was Assisi on the mountain side above us and realised that there, for better or worse, the rest of my life belonged. However inadequate and improbable I might be, people come from all over Europe to talk to me, and I must be there to receive them.

'Sadly, fumbling for words, I tried to explain this to him. He was too intelligent not to understand. Maybe he even sympathised a little. But he wouldn't accept.

' "I can't take such an answer as final," he said, "without giving you time to reflect. I am coming to Assisi with Morosino again next May. The Doge and the whole Venetian Republic is sending a full embassy to honour the remains of St Francis when they are transferred to the new basilica. I'll come to you for your answer then. So think well, Jacopa."

'And from this I couldn't budge him. We finished our meal, talking of other things, and then rode back into Assisi. Later that day he left for Venice.

'Now I find myself both dreading and longing for his return at the same time. I long to see him and I dread the necessity of confirming my refusal. And yet I must because I cannot leave this place. That is rock-like, and if I were to act contrary to it I should distort the whole pattern of things.

'So I beg you both, Giovanni and Graziano, come to Assisi next May. I greatly desire to see you both and I need you to shore up my feeble will.

Your inconstant, frail but loving mother.'

Peroni put down the manuscript thoughtfully. Jacopa presumably had remained adamant, for she had died and been buried in Assisi. But how had it gone in May? Had Michele Aquila returned? Had Giovanni and Graziano supported their mother? Had her refusal been as resolute as she intended?

The questions pounded incessantly in his mind, and one droned incessantly beneath them all like the burden of a song:

what had she looked like? The poor widow – the only description she gave of herself – matched ill with the reactions of messer Ugo and Michele Aquila. Jacopa must have been something very special indeed; it was a pity that his mind's eye could never have even the remotest notion of her.

He finished his Irish coffee and got up to re-join Dame Iolanthe.

Fresco by Torchlight

The television was booming away across the corridor, and when Peroni went in he saw that it was black and white, and transmitted in a highly irregular way with more than its fair complement of wiggly lines, zig-zag flashes and shooting stars as though somebody had just knocked it out. But the Dame was sitting four-square in front of it as though rooted, gazing into the screen with the utmost dedication. Peroni sat down to wait.

Through the strip-cartoon barrage he could make out a climber negotiating what looked like a vertical wall of rock.

'. . . . scaling one of the most formidable rock faces of Monte Cervino.' The presenter's voice sounded as though it were coming on a bad line from Australia. 'What I want to know from you is the German name for Monte Cervino, the height of this mountain, the names of its three glaciers on the Swiss side, the names of its three glaciers on the Italian side, the exact date when the summit was first reached from the Swiss side, the name of the climber and the point from which he set out, the exact date on which the summit was first reached from the Italian side, the names of the climbers and their point of departure. You have sixty seconds starting from – now!'

'Matterhorn,' said the owner of a face which loomed moon-like in concentration behind the interference, '4478 metres. The three glaciers on the Swiss side. . . .'

With an expression of mounting agony the competitor continued to pull the facts, one by one, out of his mental hat, and finally made it with half a second to go, to the frantic applause of the studio audience and Dame Iolanthe.

'Bravo!' called the Dame, 'I call that thirty million lire well earned. Well, what do you make of the letters, Commissario?'

'Absorbing,' he said, 'The only pity is that there's no picture of her. One feels – I feel that I need to see what she looked like.'

'Do you indeed?' said the Dame, giving him a curious sideways look. Then she went off at a sudden tangent. 'What do you say to a drive? I could do with a bit of fresh air myself.'

'Isn't it a bit late?' said Peroni.

'Nonsense! It'll do you good after all that shepherd's pie, won't it Alice?'

'Iolanthe is a great believer in a quick spin before bedtime.'

Reluctantly Peroni gave way, and a minute later found himself climbing into a car looking like one of those used in clown acts which erupt, belch water and smoke and eventually fall to pieces altogether.

'I deplore people who give names to their vehicles,' said the Dame, 'but in this case I couldn't resist it. I call the thing Bof, the reason being that in badly written English novels you keep on coming across characters with Battered Old Fords. Well, this is the archetypal Battered Old Ford. Hence Bof.'

The car, having first refused to start altogether, now suddenly jerked forward like a maddened mule, hurling Peroni against the windscreen.

'Sorry about that, Commissario. Alice says I ought to have seat belts fitted, but I can't stand the things.'

Coughing and spluttering like its owner smoking a Tuscan cigar, halting unpredictably every so often and occasionally appearing to take over the steering wheel itself with the most alarming results, Bof made its way out of Assisi and then started to climb Mount Subasio. After five minutes of this Peroni felt he would prefer to face half a dozen Camorra killers unarmed. After another nightmare twenty-five they came to what looked like a completely arbitrary halt.

'A little stroll,' said the Dame.

'If you don't mind I'll stay in the car, Iolanthe,' said Alice.

Peroni would have liked to do the same, but Dame Iolanthe, carrying a large torch, was disappearing up a narrow track which led steeply up from the road among trees, and she plainly expected him to follow. Grumbling inwardly, he did so.

While not quite in the Monte Cervino class, it certainly wasn't a little stroll either and Peroni, for whom the countryside was an undeveloped space between towns, found himself slipping, scrambling and out of breath. He also found himself cursing the Dame who, without word or pause, kept on ahead of him at a surprisingly fast rate. Despite whisky, cigars and high blood pressure, she must have been remarkably fit.

After what seemed to Peroni like two hours of this, they came into a sudden clearing and he saw, about fifty metres above them, standing out sharply against a velvet Umbrian night sky, what looked like a small chapel.

'The Robber's Den,' said Dame Iolanthe paradoxically, pausing for an instant and then immediately plunging on upwards.

The building, so high up that even Assisi was no more than a little nest of lights, was made of rough-hewn stone with a tiled roof. Nobody had set out to make it beautiful, but because of its sheer integrity it was. A large porch in front led to the main body of it.

'Legend has it,' said the Dame, 'that this place was once the hide-out of a notorious robber named Barnaba who, after a visit here by Francis was converted and later received into the Order. He then returned here to live a life of prayer and mortification, dying, as they say, in the odour of sanctity. This chapel was built officially in memory of Francis's passing here. Barnaba was never canonised, so it can't be in his honour of course, but people round here are very fond of him just the same, and they still call the place the robber's den. There's a statue inside which is claimed to be of him – officially quite against the rules of course – and he's said to have a way with chronic constipation.'

'Very interesting.'

Dame Iolanthe gave one of her earthy guffaws. 'I bet you're cursing me up hill and down dale,' she said disconcertingly, 'bringing you all the way up here in the middle of the night to see a disused chapel which isn't even in the guide books. And yet,' she went on with a sort of theatrical judiciousness, 'you should really be pleased. There are some fragments of fresco work here which are evidently school of Giotto. Interesting things these schools of Giotto. He came up to Assisi to do the Francis cycle in the basilica and took on a small army of local lads to help out – you know, they did the grass and the sky and maybe the trees and buildings, while he and his immediate retinue did the figures. Well, before long off they went in pursuit of another fat fee, leaving the school of behind to finish off the odds and ends, and then go on to various little jobs in the area like this. You can find work by them of all over the place. The poor chaps were stamped for life with the mark of the master so that they had to go on painting in his style without his genius. Results could be lamentable. Shall we have a look? The chapel itself is kept locked, but there are one or two bits and pieces in the porch.'

Still cursing the Dame's eccentricity which had dragged him up to the top of a mountain for a lecture on schools of, he stepped behind her over the threshold of the porch. When they were both inside she switched on her torch, and a powerful beam of light leapt unerringly up to illuminate the face of Jacopa de Settesoli.

Peroni stared in incredulous wonder. It could only be her. The style was crude, and yet by some miraculous stroke, a tiny seed of Giotto's genius must have taken root in this anonymous thirteenth century journeyman artist and produced its unique flowering in this face.

Peroni's imaginings had not even approached the reality. It was a face of transcendent simplicity, half hidden by dark hair. The features were in repose, but gave the impression that they were radiating love, and the eyes seemed to be alight with joy and the mouth on the point of breaking into laughter. The most curious thing of all, however, was that the question of whether she was beautiful or not simply didn't arise; she was herself. Peroni found this quite without precedent in his experience.

'What do you think of that, eh?' The Dame's voice seemed to come from a long way away.

'She's wonderful. . . .'

'Thought it would knock you for six.'

Peroni forced himself to look at the fresco analytically. It was over the door and showed the miniature figure of Jacopa kneeling, hands joined in prayer, at the feet of a much larger

89

figure, wooden and lifeless, that was plainly intended to be Francis. Slowly an objection occurred to Peroni.

'How do we know that it's meant to be her?' he asked.

'I wondered when you'd get round to asking that,' said the Dame, who sounded very pleased with herself. '*You* know that it's meant to be her because it's the only face in the world that could possibly belong to the woman who wrote those letters. But I came to it in a slightly more roundabout way. I happened to be up here for a tramp one day last spring when it suddenly came on to rain, so I took shelter in here. The fresco was in much worse condition then than it is now. For one thing Jacopa's head was missing altogether. Been plastered over by some fool. All I could tell was that it was a small female figure kneeling. Nothing remarkable about that. You get these kneeling suppliants in a lot of medieval work, sculpture as well as painting. But then I realised that there was a detail about it which should have been telling me something, but it was a second before I understood what it was. It was that!'

With finely timed theatricality, Dame Iolanthe centred the beam of her torch onto the woman's cloak. Peroni saw what looked like a large T more or less over the heart.

'The tau cross,' said the Dame, 'tau being the Greek for T. St Francis had a particular devotion for the tau cross. You remember Jacopa's letter? "The only outward concession that I make to his memory is that I always have a tau cross sewn on my cloak." Well, I reckoned there can't have been many women going about Assisi with a tau cross on their cloaks and still less who would be likely to be painted with Francis. Ergo, my dear Commissario, it had to be Jacopa. I got in touch with Commendator Palanca, the Superintendent of Fine Arts here.'

'I know him.'

'Oh yes, of course, you're both from the same neck of the woods, aren't you? Splendid chap. He came up and had a look straight away and said he thought something could be done about it, and less than a month later experts were already at work. This is the result.'

Peroni felt guilty about the mental abuse he had hurled at Dame Iolanthe. 'It was very kind of you indeed to bring me up here,' he said sincerely, in an attempt at partial reparation.

'I thought you'd be pleased,' she said, 'It's always satisfactory to be able to see the face of a person one's in love with.' She lit a Tuscan cigar and gave him another of her odd sideways looks. 'Time we were getting back to Alice and Bof.'

Burrowing Deeper into the Past

'We're having lunch with Rocco today,' Assunta announced over coffee the next morning. 'At the Excelsior,' she underlined.

The passing of time had not rendered the prospect of this any more appealing. She foresaw an hour of platitudes and pomposity as her brother and Rocco played their respective roles of Commissario of Police and Superintendent of Fine Arts. Even Achille himself didn't seem any too enthusiastic about it. Come to that, it almost looked as though her announcement hadn't got through to him at all.

'Um?' he said, confirming this impression, 'What's that?'

'Our lunch with Rocco,' she said, 'It's today.'

'Our lunch with Rocco,' he repeated, but the words plainly meant nothing to him.

She examined him curiously, then with alarm. He was looking distinctly haggard. 'Are you all right, Achille?' she enquired.

'What? Oh yes, I'm perfectly all right.'

A thought struck her. 'Did you go to hospital yesterday?'

'Hospital? Why should I go to hospital?'

'Your hand!'

'Oh no – I forgot all about it. I'm following up something which may —'

'You must be out of your mind! If that hand gets infected, it could be serious.'

'I'll go today. I must just look through some books first.'

'Books?'

'I was trying to tell you – I'm onto something which might be very important indeed.'

'Concerning Signora Guidi?'

91

'Well, that was the start of it, but it's a lot more complicated than that.' His tiredness suddenly looked accentuated. 'I'll probably never get it sorted out.'

'Achille,' said Assunta, 'I suppose you realise this could be dangerous?'

'My hand, you mean?'

'I'm talking about something else now. You've got no authorisation to go round making enquiries. Heaven knows what they might not cook up if they found out. You know how mean and ruthless people can be if they get a sniff of something like that – particularly if you were involved. There must be an awful lot of your colleagues who'd give anything to get the Rudolph Valentino of the Italian police into trouble.'

'You don't need to worry about me.'

'I wish I could be sure of that.' Another idea occurred to her. 'I suppose by any chance there's not another woman involved in all this?'

Accustomed as she was to interpreting his expressions, there was something about the one he now wore which she found quite undecipherable.

'I wish it could be put as simply as that,' he said, 'but it can't.'

'Well anyway, don't forget to have that hand looked at.'

What vital fact had Lorenzo Florio-Levi unearthed about the doings in Assisi in 1230? Assuming, as Peroni was increasingly inclined to do, that his death was the result of his passionate pilgrimage into the past, then that death itself was a clear indication that he had discovered some such fact.

But what? What could conceivably have happened more than seven hundred years ago to spring a murder in twentieth century Assisi? Something in which Jacopa de Settesoli had apparently been centrally involved.

The two addresses which had led him to Signora Rosalba and Dame Iolanthe had seemed to be a major breakthrough, but now – although Jacopa had become almost more alive for him than a woman of flesh and blood – he was no further forward with the central problem of Lorenzo's death.

Sorting through all this endlessly in his mind during the night,

92

Peroni had come to the conclusion that the only course open to him was to go conscientiously through the books in Lorenzo's apartment. In all that historical earth there might be one or two radium-grams of truth. So now, having made his way once more to the Florio-Levi works and crossed the floor under the openly curious gaze of the gnomes, he found himself once again in the nice secretary's office.

'*Buon giorno,*' she said, sounding pleased to see him.

'I can't go on thinking of you as the nice secretary,' he said, 'I'd much prefer to know your name.'

'Bonato,' she said, 'Raffaella Bonato. But didn't you see it in your colleague's report?'

That, thought Peroni, was a quite exceptionally stupid mistake. He could have glossed it over with a vague 'Oh yes, of course', but for some reason felt a strong aversion for lying to her. 'I haven't read my colleague's report,' he said, 'Things aren't exactly what they seem to be.'

'Oh?' Interested, amused, waiting for more.

'I'm a Commissario of police all right, but I'm not stationed here in Perugia. I've got no authority to be enquiring into this business.'

'And that's bad?'

'Very bad indeed. If I were taking massive hand-outs from the Camorra nobody would mind particularly, but incorrectnesses like this are severely frowned on.'

She smiled, then looked serious. 'But why are you enquiring into it?'

'I hardly know myself. I'm on leave and I happened to be a member of Signora Guidi's pilgrimage. When she was arrested on Wednesday I found myself just not believing she was guilty. I thought her story was true.'

Sudden alarm flared in Raffaella's eyes. She had it under control at once, but it had been unmistakable. She carefully adjusted a sheet of paper in the typewriter. 'You must have good reason for thinking that.'

'Not really. Or not to begin with anyway. But maybe I'm beginning to get an idea of the sort of thing he was murdered about.'

'And what can I do to help you?'

'You don't mind helping me?'

She thought. 'It's no good trying to stop the truth. What can I do?'

'I want to have another look through Lorenzo's books.'

'Go ahead. You know the way.'

Peroni stood up. 'You've been very kind.'

She seemed uncertain about something. 'There's just one thing. . . .'

'Yes?'

'It's probably of no importance, but – well, a few days ago I lost a key to this building. I usually carry two. This was the spare.'

'So if somebody else was in this building on Tuesday night, they could have got in with that key?'

'It's possible.' She didn't like the idea.

'Where did you lose it?'

'Could be in any one of a dozen places.'

'Where did you carry it?'

'In my bag.'

'Could anyone have taken it from your bag?'

The telephone rang, and she seemed relieved at the interruption. She talked for several minutes about package and delivery of glass, taking notes in deft shorthand.

'Did you tell the investigating officer from Perugia about this key?'

'No. I didn't realise that I'd lost it then.'

'Who knew that you carried a spare key?'

She was on the point of saying something and then apparently changed her mind. 'Look,' she substituted, 'I must get on with this order now. I've got a busy day. Do you mind if we put off this talk till later?'

In view of his confessed unofficiality, Peroni could hardly protest. 'What time do you finish here?'

'Seven o'clock.'

'Can I meet you then?'

'That'll be fine. Help yourself to the books.'

He had the impression that she was relieved, now, to be

rid of him.

The mere sight of the book was alarming. It was a ponderous bibliographical blunderbuss, quite sufficient to batter someone to death. Its binding was an uncompromising black as though it were in mourning for its contents. But if the sight of it was alarming, its title was even more so. *An Historical Survey of Assisium or Ascesi*, it announced in what would have been a professorial drone if it had had a voice, *from its Prehistoric Origins in the Villanovian age to the present day, taking into account the Etruscan Domination, the subsequent Roman conquest with the City's passage to the status of Municipium, the Barbaric Invasions and subsequent Longobard Rule, followed by the Struggle against Feudalism and long Ghibelline Tradition, and containing also a detailed Topological Study of the City and its immediate surroundings together with exhaustive Geological, Architectural and Archeological Considerations and Abundant Surveys of the Flora and Fauna on Monte Subasio.*

This monument to sheer staying power had been published in the 1880s, and Peroni had chosen it, having no other criterion, because it was the biggest in Lorenzo's collection. He opened the front cover which put him in mind of a prison gate and started to look for the thirteenth century.

When he got there, he found himself stuck, like a speed boat in a mud-bank, in the Guelf-Ghibelline conflict with which Assisi was heavily involved. He was on the point of giving it up as a bad job and trying a less formidable volume when he suddenly found himself in an unexpected clearing in the political jungle.

'In the Year of Grace 1230,' he read, 'an Event of extreme notability occurred, nay, two Events, for the one was the progenitor of the other, and a great Concourse of People from all the Italic Land, and many other people from lands throughout the globe, thronged to Assisi to be present at these Events: to wit, the opening of the Lower of the two churches which today comprise the Universally Admired Basilica of San Francesco and the transfer of the Mortal Remains of the Great Thaumaturge to the Crypt of that same Edifice where they lie today from the Church of San Giorgio wherein they had hitherto been housed until the accomplishment of Brother Elias's Monumental Edifice.'

With the feeling that he just might be onto something, Peroni nosed his way through the sluggish prose, but when he had reached the end of the description and the author had got back to his Guelfs and Ghibellines, he found he was no better off. The facts were still two: the Lower church had been opened, and the body of St Francis had been transferred there from San Giorgio.

He lowered the *Historical Survey* back where it had come from and tried again, but the next half dozen books which he fished out in this improbable lucky dip did no more than confirm that Lorenzo was studying thirteenth century Assisi.

The eighth volume was slimmer than its predecessors, but didn't look much more promising. 'An Extract from the Government Accounts of the Serenissima Republic,' said the title page, and in fact the book was little more than a series of lists containing the names of people involved on various errands for the Venetian Republic to Padua, Milan and other city states together with the amounts disbursed in ducats. He was about to put it back when a name suddenly jumped out at him from the head of a list.

Bartolomeo Morosino. The man, Michele Aquila had told Jacopa, who had headed the Venetian embassy to Assisi. The date was right, he noticed with rising excitement, May 1230, and in the five names that immediately followed Morosino's was that of Michele himself. These six men had been accompanied by twenty-five outriders, guards and bearers.

The trail that Lorenzo had followed was once again clear, but everything was still impenetrable in the direction it led. This was the visit Michele had promised Jacopa. What had passed between them? And what bearing did it have on Lorenzo's search seven hundred years afterwards?

Peroni attacked the books with renewed enthusiasm, but he struck another bad patch. Volumes and volumes of history, all covering more or less the same period, but none of them, so far as he could tell from selective dips, reporting anything he didn't already know.

Finally he came to the last book. It had been printed in 1935 and bore the title *Venetian Portraits*, and the list of contents showed immediately what it was doing there, for one of the portraits was of Bartolomeo Morosino. Peroni turned to it.

'There is a painting of Bartolomeo Morosino in the Doge's palace,' it said, 'and a glance at it is sufficient to show why this man was so highly valued by the Republic. The face is thin, highly intelligent, with clear marks of ruthlessness. The nose is long, the mouth hard, and the eyes those of a marauding hawk. If one could give a single face to Venetian politics in the first half of the thirteenth century, this would be it.

'The tremendous explosion of trade which, in an incredibly short space of time, made the Republic the richest in Europe, owed much to him, his embassies in the east, particularly Constantinople, being the invariable prelude to contracts and deals that would make even the most ambitious of present-day businessmen boggle.

'But for all its outstanding qualities, the face of Bartolomeo Morosino is not one to please women. From all one is able to glean of his private life, however, this will not have distressed him greatly, for he was unmarried and regarded the opposite sex with extreme contempt.

'This contempt, it would seem, did not extend to younger members of his own sex, and he is said to have had a marked preference for young men of Teutonic origin. In fact, contemporary records show that his retinues usually included a German aide or guard.

'Morosino's total eclipse from the Venetian political scene is generally ascribed to his sudden death as a result of illness. The facts, however, are by no means clear and there is no conclusive evidence. In the view of the present writer, however, it is not impossible that he had some form of disagreement with the dreaded Council of Three as a result of which he went into rapid, voluntary exile. And if he had not been so shrewd and experienced a politician, one would also have to consider the hypothesis that he was made to disappear.

'His career began in the last decade of the twelfth century. . . .'

There was nothing more of specific interest and no mention of the mission to Assisi. After a second's thought, Peroni got a sheet of paper and wrote down the names of the characters involved. Jacopa herself and her two sons, Giovanni and Graziano; Morosino and Michele Aquila; two friars – the hustling, unpleasant and unstoppable Elias and the gentle, mystical Giles; the Captain of the People, messer Ugo, and his wife; the rubicund town crier Ilario. Ten characters.

No, wait, maybe there was an eleventh. The portrait of Morosino had pointed at the presence of a young German. Peroni went back to the Extract from the Government Accounts and ran through the list of names once again. Corrado di Turingia. Clearly of German origin. Peroni added the name to his list.

Eleven characters then, and the setting was still there all about him, practically unchanged from the thirteenth century when they had acted out their drama in it. But just what was their drama? Pirandello had written *Six Characters in Search of an Author*: Peroni was now faced with eleven characters in search of a script. If there was a script that united them all. He looked through the list again, and it occurred to him that if he checked the names in the indexes of the various books, he might turn up something that had escaped him. It was a tedious job, but after twenty minutes it produced a result.

Looking up Ilario the rubicund in the massive tome where he had started his research he came across an acknowledgement. The author, it said, wished to thank Signorina Zuzzi, daughter of the late Prof. Zuzzi for her courtesy in allowing him to look through her father's manuscript collection of the *Chronicles of Ilario the rubicund*. This was clearly the missing collection that Lorenzo had ordered himself to trace.

The phone book listed only one Zuzzi in Assisi, a certain *dott.* Ottavio, but he turned out to be the right one and, what was more, available.

'I can only tell you,' he said when Peroni had put the question, 'what I told Signor Florio-Levi when he asked me the same thing earlier this year. My grandmother donated the collection to the library of the Friars Minor here in Assisi.'

Brother Giles's Blood

'We are facing an extremely grave crisis in left-wing relationships, motivated not by ideological abstractions but by conflicts
concerning the conception and futurability of union and Party
cohesion in the multiple. . . .'

But for some reason the leading article of *Unità*, the daily organ
of the Italian Communist Party, was not absorbing Commissario
Zanetti's attention as much as it usually did. The reason, of
course, was that bourgeois affair in Assisi. There was something
indefinably wrong about it. Everything indicated that Signora
Guidi had shot Lorenzo Florio-Levi, and yet Zanetti was worried.
His experience told him that a politically illiterate woman would
break down immediately under systematic interrogation, but by
now she had been in custody for more than thirty-six hours and
she was still insisting that Florio-Levi had been alive when she
left him.

And to make matters worse her husband, who was a lawyer –
apparently indifferent to the horns his wife and Florio-Levi had
planted on his forehead – was arousing a hurricane of protest in
Perugia.

He forced his concentration back onto *Unità*. 'The analysis of
objective and subjective novelties within the Party should be put
into relief in order to examine the state of the workers' movement
in its political, trade union and cultural manifestations. . . .'

The telephone rang on Zanetti's desk and he picked it up with
irritation. 'Zanetti.'

'An outside caller wants to speak to you, *dottore*. He refuses to
give his name, but says he has information concerning the Assisi
killing.'

'Put him through.' A brief pause and a click.

'Commissario Zanetti?'

'Who's speaking?'

'It doesn't matter who I am. I have information that may be of
interest to you.'

The voice could have been a light male one or a heavy female one; in either case, it was almost certainly in some way distorted.

'What is it?'

'There's a man making enquiries in Assisi who wrongfully purports to come from the police. He's been questioning people at the Florio-Levi works.'

The receiver was put down at the other end. Zanetti looked helplessly at *Unità* in search of inspiration. FASCIST HARASS-MENT, said a headline. It could hardly have been put better.

Peroni had a strong sense of having been there before, maybe in a dream. He recognised those endless, echoing, polished corridors which seemed to be part of an enormous maze, the huge mosaics and pictures which all seemed to be nineteenth century. He remembered the dimness of it all and the silence and the institutional smells, among which last night's supper cavorted stubbornly with today's lunch. But in the dream he had been alone, whereas now he was accompanied by a friar who was discoursing amiably about football.

'What a match! There hasn't been one like it since the world cup! Although, of course,' he added hastily as Franciscan courtesy got the upper hand of football fever, 'being a Naples supporter you'll be prejudiced.'

'No, no,' said Peroni generously without adding that football left him so indifferent he didn't even follow the fortunes of his own home team.

'Well, that's wise of you, too,' said the friar as though Peroni had scored a neat theological point. 'Mark you, I'm all for patriotism in football, but not for chauvinism – it spoils everything if you can't appreciate any team except your own. Here we are.'

The last sentence sounded such an inherent part of the rest that Peroni almost expected to find himself being led into a stadium. The friar, using one of the keys that hung from the white cord round his waist, bent down to unlock a door and then, standing aside, let Peroni pass into a room which, as far as he could gauge its size in the darkness might well indeed have been a stadium. But then the friar switched on the lights, and the supporters,

100

massed densely around in rows, were all revealed to be books.

'Now then, Ilario the rubicund,' said the friar opening a file, 'You say we have a manuscript of extracts from the *Chronicles*. I can't say I've ever come across it myself, but we have a mass of stuff that gets donated and then never looked at again.'

'This was looked at once earlier this year.'

'Was it indeed? Somebody else must have supervised the loan then. Ah, here we are. Ilario the rubicund, *Chronicles*, extracts from, MS, donated Zuzzi 1889, Col. SR 395. Sit down, won't you? It may take me a little while to run it down.'

But within a few minutes he was back, dusty, dishevelled and triumphant, waving a small volume as if it had been a silver cup. 'Here we are!' he said. 'Easier to locate than I expected. Now you just take your time, and I'll be about if there's anything you want.' Saying this he set off towards the distant recesses of the library at a pace which looked suspiciously as though he were dribbling an invisible ball.

Peroni opened the manuscript, which had been bound in a leather cover. He started to examine the ornate, sloping handwriting. Ilario's reputation for scurrility was quickly borne out; if one were to believe him, thirteenth century Assisi was as dense with every conceivable variety of heinous sin as Dante's Hell. After skidding rapidly over this sea of depravity for about quarter of an hour, Peroni spotted the name Francis, so he went back to the beginning of the verse and started to chip it out word by word.

And now when in these days
From Heaven Francis surveys
The removal of his bones
To the charnel house of stones
Erected by that Friar Elias
Whose brothers are all solemn liars,
The sun shines bright upon the concourse
Of hypocrites and thieves and whores.
But now the sinners for a change
Aren't merely local ones – they range
From Roman pigs and lust-filled Grecians

101

To Florentines and, worse, Venetians,
The train of whose ambassador
Contains no women, but one whore.

Something in Peroni's brain went very taut, like a wire suddenly taking the strain of weight.

This train is lodged in the lesser tower
Where strange events begin to flower,
For although six go in alive,
The ones who go away are five.
Corrado named di Turingia
Is luckless sixth, so hears this singer.

So the eleven characters did have a script after all. Peroni sat back in his chair and stared at the situation as though it were hovering on the air before him. The lesser tower. That could only be the one where Signora Guidi had been arrested, and a murder there would account for the wild-cat clawing of the past which Peroni had undergone in the upper chamber.

For what possible motive would Corrado have been killed? Obviously the lover of a man like Morosino was in a dangerous position. Corrado might have discovered Venetian state secrets and tried to sell them. Or he might have gained information about Morosino himself and threatened to use it against him. Peroni's mind raced along half a dozen tracks of possible medieval intrigue in high places and then, like a dog suddenly realising the folly of chasing butterflies, came to a halt. It was useless speculating without more evidence.

But one thing was now surely beyond dispute. The murder of Corrado must have figured in some way in Lorenzo's quest into the past. He had gone rummaging there for his thesis and come across this. And then? Well, then presumably he would have continued searching the *Chronicles*. Peroni decided to do the same.

Because Professor Zuzzi had only been able to collect extracts they were inevitably disconnected, and events appeared starkly out of context like fragments of a mosaic. But there were various indications of passing time, and Peroni began to feel that the vital

102

1230 must by now have been left some way behind. He was on the point of abandoning the search when he spotted another familiar name.

It was absurd. He felt like an adolescent coming unexpectedly on the name of a girl he loves. And then he remembered the curious observation Dame Iolanthe had made about the fresco in the robber's den.

The reference was at the very bottom of a page.

> Jacopa, she of the Seven Suns
> Was always one of the wilder ones—

Peroni turned the page to continue.

> Tapping the wine, and when that was done
> Replacing with piss the wine that was gone.

He stared at the page. He had been prepared for scandal, abuse, but this was just nonsense. And then, reading ahead a couple of lines, he saw the reason: Ilario was no longer talking about Jacopa at all, but about a fraudulent merchant. Why then was the piece about her so abruptly interrupted? He turned back to the previous page in search of inspiration and got none. It was only when he looked between the pages that he saw what had happened.

One page had been neatly removed.

A Mystery Defined

Having parked near the basilica of Santa Chiara, Scansani walked along Corso Mazzini towards the centre. Assisi was at its May best with a brilliant blue sky and pennants fluttering on a gentle Umbrian breeze. Here and there were figures in medieval dress making the scene even brighter, and the tourists milled about them clicking their cameras and calling and exclaiming in half a dozen foreign languages like an aviary full of over-excited

103

parrots. And the dresses of the girls were as dazzling as the pennants.

Scansani felt as isolated as a ghost at a wedding. The girls perturbed him dreadfully. He was somewhat fat and had a bulbous nose with a cleft in the middle from which there sprouted little hairs, and above this his eyebrows met in the middle giving him a cross air. He also suffered from premature baldness and bad breath. For all these reasons he was not attractive to women, a fact which didn't prevent them being very attractive to him, so that displays of nubility such as Assisi offered this morning troubled him badly. He usually tried to relieve this by immersing himself in work, but this wasn't having its usual effect, perhaps because the job he was engaged on seemed to have neither head nor tail to it.

Reaching the Piazza del Comune, he decided a beer might help, but unfortunately when he had sat down outside a *caffe* he realised that the girl who was waiting at the tables was every bit as attractive as the ones in Corso Mazzini: modest looking (which made it worse) with long dark hair and quick eyes. He pulled up thoughts of work about him like the collar of a mackintosh in a rainstorm.

Commissario Zanetti had received an anonymous call to say that somebody, posing as a policeman, had been going round asking questions about the Florio-Levi assassination and he, Scansani, had been deputed to track that person down. There were various disadvantages to this. For one thing the call, like most anonymous calls, was probably a hoax. For another, even if it wasn't, the phony policeman would have to be some sort of lunatic, for nobody in their right senses would have run such a stupid risk. And then there was the problem of how to find out.

These thoughts evaporated instantly as Scansani realised that the waitress was coming towards him. Only to take his order, of course, but there was a little smile on her face which suggested that she didn't find the task altogether disagreeable. Hope staggered to its feet for the umpteenth time; here at last was she who could see through appearance to reality.

And then, with the half smile still on her face, the girl walked straight past him as though he hadn't been there at all. Hope went down once more for the count as he followed her progress. She stopped in front of another single man. A southerner, unjustly good-looking with perfectly even, very white teeth which showed in the answering smile that he was giving the girl.

Scansani looked at him with loathing.

Peroni's smile was quite genuine. In spite of the image of Jacopa which dominated his mind, he couldn't help appreciating the girl who had come for his order. Local beauty she had that went with olive trees and wayside shrines and dusty tracks in the sun.

'*Si, signore?*'

'*Un Campari Soda, per piacere.*' It was a Campari Soda morning.

She smiled again and went, leaving Peroni to mull over thoughts of his find in the monastery library. The exhilaration of it was still with him. His reasoning had been correct. He had been right in the teeth of the evidence and the Perugia police had been wrong. What a sensation it would create in the media!

But then his tide of exhilaration began to ebb. Without the missing page, the sensation could never be achieved, and the chances of finding it were negligible. The withdrawing exhilaration left behind a soggy foreshore of gloom.

He perked up a little at the sight of the girl emerging from the bar with his drink, which she deposited on his table before another exchange of smiles and a modest retreat.

Taking a chilly sip of Campari, Peroni became aware that somebody was staring at him. Without appearing to do so, he glanced in the direction from which the stare was coming and saw a woebegone-looking man with a nose shaped like an electric light bulb. This man was clearly looking at him with dislike, and yet the chaotic archives of Peroni's mind could produce no information about him. Just the same there was something. Something like a not particularly pleasant but long familiar smell. It took Peroni about a tenth of a second to place it.

The man was a policeman.

Peroni eyed him covertly, wondering whether he had something to do with the Florio-Levi enquiry and, if so, what. But after a minute, the man finished his beer, put some money on the table and left. Peroni looked at his watch. There was still some time before the lunch date with Rocco, and a throbbing in his left hand made him decide it would be wise to employ it on a visit to hospital. He picked up the bill.

'None the worse for your midnight mountaineering I see, Commissario.'

The glass on the table before him vibrated to the sound of Dame Iolanthe's voice. He rose to meet her. Her appearance today was enhanced by a large floppy-brimmed hat and a silver-topped walking stick.

'Campari Soda?' she said, accepting his invitation to sit. 'Yes, I'll have that, too, with a drop of vodka. They say Campari is the most delicious of all the aperitifs and the most punishing for the liver. And talking of aperitifs, have you ever reflected, Commissario, that the number of different varieties there are in Italy is only equalled by the number of different political parties? There must be some connection between the two things, but I've never been able to work out what it is. Would it be imprudent to ask how your enquiry is progressing?'

'I expect it would,' said Peroni, 'but I shall be delighted to tell you just the same.'

The Neapolitan showman in him, in fact, jumped at the opportunity for a display of virtuosity and at the same time he was pleased at the chance she offered him to sort out his ideas.

'I am,' she said, 'as the phrase has it, all ears.'

'You remember how Brother Giles foretold blood?'

'I do.' She held her glass up in silent salute and for an instant it seemed to be a chalice of blood.

'Well, now I think I know what he meant. There was a murder in Assisi in May 1230.'

The Neapolitan showman could not have hoped for a more spectacular reaction. The Dame goggled and her mouth dropped open. 'A murder?' she said. 'This is too good to be true! Tell on.'

Peroni told on, and she followed the story like an impressionable child at a puppet show. When it was done she whistled reverently. 'One up to you, Commissario – not to say half a dozen. As fine a piece of historical sleuthing as ever I came across in my life. Of course, I *knew* about Ilario, too, but I never followed him up that far. So young Florio-Levi knocked off a page of the manuscript, eh? And the next question, presumably, is why.'

'Exactly. And the only possible indication lies in the switch of Lorenzo's attention from Ilario to Jacopa. I tried to work out the order in which things must have happened, and this was fairly helpful in a negative sort of way. First of all Lorenzo was assigned a thesis on Ilario the rubicund – the date of that can be checked. He then proceeded to get hold of books dealing with the period in general, and in one of these he found an acknowledgement giving the identity of the anonymous nineteenth century scholar who had collected extracts from the *Chronicles*. He contacted the family and found that the manuscript had been donated to the library of the Friars Minor. And this led him to the murder of Corrado and – well, the missing page. From then on he virtually abandoned the thesis and concentrated on Jacopa instead.'

'Mm,' said the Dame pensively snorting into her vodka-Campari, 'and once again, why did he purloin the page? Because the contents were in some way useful or helpful? No, no, no.' She cocked at Peroni the ironically humorous look of a chess-player side-stepping a false move which his opponent expects him to make. 'He could have copied it without any trouble.' She and Peroni exchanged almost conspiratorial nods. 'That leaves just one possibility then. He wanted to be absolutely certain that nobody else should see that page.'

'My view, too,' said Peroni. 'And so that page probably contains the key to the whole thing. It establishes the link between May 1230 and today, between Corrado and Lorenzo. The deduction, so far as it goes, is perfect but, without knowing what was written there, that isn't a great deal of help.'

The Dame went into a trance at this, humming tunelessly and rocking backwards and forwards on the two back legs of her chair. After this had been going on for some while she stopped and took a long, meditative pull at her Tuscan cigar. She then opened her mouth, and Peroni waited reverently for a pronouncement, but instead she was taken by a violent fit of coughing, and only after a great deal of vodka and Campari alternated with vigorous back-slapping, which she mutely enjoined Peroni to administer, was she ready to utter. She allowed suspense to build

107

up once again and then pronounced the single word, 'Something.'

'I beg your pardon?' said Peroni.

'Something,' she repeated, 'as opposed to Somebody. Generations of Somebodies have died since then, so it's reasonable to rule out any direct human link. But Somethings last. Seven hundred years is nothing for a Something.'

Peroni looked at her with some veneration, reflecting that such a first class piece of reasoning ought to have come from him. But then he began to wonder whether she hadn't merely shifted the emphasis of the problem.

'You're quite right,' he said, 'but the nature of the Something is still a mystery.'

'A French Dominican whose name escapes me,' began Dame Iolanthe surprisingly and somewhat sententiously, 'once defined a mystery as something dark in itself which sheds light on everything around it. That, Commissario, is the sort of mystery that you have on your hands now.'

Shameful Behaviour at a Luncheon Party

The Excelsior, thought Assunta, looked its name. It was all gleaming cutlery, snow-white tablecloths and shining crystal. The waiters were as obsequiously unobtrusive as high class undertakers, and the hushed voices and solemn tones of the customers suggested that they were mourners at the funeral.

And there in the middle of it, in perfect harmony with the setting, was Rocco, rising to meet her.

'My dear Assunta, how pleasant to see you.' As he took her hand, she noticed costly links glide out of his cuff like a Rolls from its garage. 'And where is Achille?'

'I think he went to hospital to have his hand dressed. He'll turn up.'

'Perhaps you'll join me in a glass of sherry while we wait?'

Oh, *santo cielo*! sherry, thought Assunta, that's all we needed.

'Thank you,' she said aloud. And as they sipped the stuff, exchanging pleasantries, she reflected that the worst of it was that there was no rebelling against these things. Like menstruation and death you just had to accept them.

'Ah, here is Achille,' she said after a while with some relief.

The two men shook hands like heads of state. 'Assunta and I are having sherry, Achille.'

'I'll stick to Campari, if you don't mind.'

Rocco murmured instructions to a waiter and then studied one of his cuff-links as a pause fell on the three musketeers.

'Assisi must be a prize job for a Superintendent of Fine Arts,' said Achille.

'It involves a great deal of work,' said Rocco. 'And what about Venice for a Commissario of Police?'

'I'm afraid it's rather like being a detective in a museum,' said Peroni, adding hastily, 'Meaning no disrespect to museums, of course.'

'No, no, of course not – I quite take your point.'

Another heavy pause fell, to be finally broken this time by Rocco.

'I daresay you're *au fait* with our murder.' He made it sound like a garden party. 'Quite unusual for Assisi.'

'I've been following it.'

'And what is your – um, professional view of the affair?'

'I don't really know sufficient to form an opinion.'

'Ye–e–e–s,' Rocco drawled the monosyllable, 'I quite see that.' He sipped his sherry. 'Remarkable family, the Florio-Levis.'

'You know them?'

'I've been in touch – because of stained glass, you see.'

'Ah yes, naturally.'

'And the young man – what was his name? Lorenzo – came to see me about a month ago concerning some thesis he was doing. Wanted to know about a thirteenth century character called Jacopa de Settesoli.'

It seemed to Assunta that interest flickered somewhere inside her brother's apathy.

'Were you able to tell him anything?'

'I gave him a couple of addresses. One of a house she was supposed to have lived in, and the other of an eccentric English woman here in Assisi who is supposed to be writing a biography

109

of her. That was the last I saw of him.'

Now Assunta thought she could detect a gleam of satisfaction in her brother's eyes as though something had been cleared up.

'I understand,' went on Rocco, 'that they're holding the funeral on Monday.'

'We shall be back in Verona by then.'

'Yes, of course. Well, I daresay you're feeling peckish, so let's order.' They were given menus as big as billboards, and Rocco steered them through the niceties of Umbrian food and wine as though they'd been a couple of visiting ministers. Assunta noticed that the waiter addressed him as Commendatore, and as soon as the ordering was done, Peroni took up the point, perhaps, she suspected, with a touch of envy.

'So you're a Commendatore, Rocco?'

'Oh, it's one of those things that tend to go with the job,' said Rocco looking at his other cuff-link. 'Oh, by the way,' he went on, 'I was given these this morning and as I can't use them myself, I thought you might care to. They're invitations to a helicopter flight over the city and surrounding area on Saturday afternoon. It's a May Day event for VIPs organised by the municipality.'

He took it for granted, Assunta noticed, that he was a VIP himself. And to think, she reflected, that I was once passionately in love with this world champion of self-importance. 'How kind of you,' she said.

At this point they were interrupted by a hushed but vibrant female voice. 'Commendator Palanca!' it said, sounding as though its owner were at a papal audience. 'What a felicitous surprise!'

The two men stood up and Rocco, more urbane and distinguished than ever, introduced Peroni and Assunta.

'A Commissario of Police!' murmured the lady, dramatically switching the beam of her admiration full on Peroni. 'How reassuring to meet a man of moral integrity! This is what I always say to Commendator Palanca – and I assure you it's no joking matter nowadays, particularly in a place like Assisi where we get every sort of rag-tag and bobtail, taking drugs and playing guitars. Indeed, one comes across many seemingly respectable people only to find out the most outrageous things about them

110

afterwards.'

Seated, cupping a glass of wine, Assunta looked up in despair at the two men. They actually believed what the woman was saying. Achille and Rocco – who had run through the whole *scugnizzo* spectrum of highly-coloured sins – found nothing ridiculous or even inappropriate in this vision of themselves as pillars of moral integrity.

'I tell you in all seriousness,' the lady continued, 'I have often felt obliged to go and wash my hands on learning of the actions of some of the people I have shaken hands with. Nowadays anyone may have been anything!'

Practically the first thing Assunta had noticed about Rocco when she had come across him in the basilica three days earlier had been the complicated, apparently haphazard network of lines with which his face was scored. And now all these lines seemed to be vibrating, as though charged with some powerful but undefined emotion. 'Even,' he said, 'a Superintendent of Fine Arts?'

Suddenly, to her incredulous delight, Assunta realised that what the lines were charged with was laughter. It was not yet explicit, but it was a powerful spring working its way towards the surface.

'Even,' said her brother, 'a Commissario of Police?'

Delight redoubled when she saw that Achille had caught the infection, too.

'Ah no,' said the lady archly, 'certain people are exceptions. I can always tell. You, my dear Commissario, you, Commendatore – and you, too, Signora,' she went on as an afterthought, turning to Assunta, 'you are transparent. One can see that you have never committed dishonest or shameful actions. My instinct for these things is infallible.'

The spring had become a gusher, and now it broke as the two of them burst into uncontrollable laughter, joined by Assunta. The lady was taken aback by this violent display of hilarity, but after a second, deciding it must be a result of her own unconscious humour, she joined in a little nervously. Assunta, Rocco and Peroni were powerless in the blast of it, and the lady continued to participate gingerly. Finally, as the gush gave no signs of abating, she reversed into a tentative smile and said, 'I'm afraid I must be going now.'

'I hope,' said Rocco, 'you won't bother to waste good soap on us.'

At this alarm took over her features completely. She backed a few steps, then turned and made off in a panicky waddle.

Rocco and Achille collapsed in their chairs in the grip of a force stronger then themselves, unaware that they were being observed all round with expressions ranging from disapproval to horror.

'Waiter,' called Rocco in a voice more suited to a cheap *osteria* than the Excelsior restaurant, 'bring us a couple of litre jugs of white wine!' And when they came, he topped up, not the wine glasses, but the larger ones intended for water. No Superintendent of Fine Arts in his right mind would have done that, thought Assunta with delight. Then he compounded the offence by getting out a packet of filterless Nazionali cigarettes, the cheapest and roughest brand on the market, which they all three used to smoke in the old days.

'I always carry these bloody things around with me,' he said, lighting for all three of them. 'They're the only cigarettes I like, but I never have the nerve to smoke them except in the lavatory. Chin chin!'

With the almost ritual solemnity of three musketeers meeting up at last, they downed the wine in one and he filled up the glasses again.

'Everybody's looking at us,' said Assunta.

'I don't give a bugger,' said Rocco.

'Let's hope they enjoy themselves,' said Achille.

Assunta's cup of happiness was full.

'I feel,' said Peroni, 'as though I'd taken a very powerful laxative after several years of constipation.'

Tentatively, as though to visitors from outer space, the food was served them, and as they ate they started to talk about the past. They drank so much wine that Assunta lost count of the number of jugs and remarked with an un-ladylike giggle that back in Verona she would have made observations if there had been more than one.

'But why a pilgrimage?' said Rocco at some point. 'Given my

position, I'm obliged to forgive you yours. But a package deal pilgrimage! I would never have thought it of you, Achille.'

'It was her fault,' said Peroni, sounding like Adam explaining about the apple.

'*Madonna santissima!*' she said as Rocco turned to her, 'I needed to get away! Do you mind? Some women can go for cruises or skiing holidays. I was offered a package deal pilgrimage. Either eat the soup or jump out of the window. I took it.'

'And what have you been doing since you got here?'

'*I've* been looking at buildings. He,' she jutted her chin at Peroni, 'started off by chasing the woman who shot the stained-glass man. Ever since she was arrested he's been nosing.'

'So you do know something about it after all?' said Rocco wagging a reproachful finger beneath Peroni's nose. 'Crafty sod!'

'I didn't feel like confiding in a Superintendent of Fine Arts.'

'He says,' said Assunta, 'that even if Signora Guidi had shot at him, she would have missed.'

Rocco laughed raucously. 'That makes sense, though I doubt if it would be accepted in court.'

'What else have you got to go on, Achille?' Assunta asked curiously. 'You said you were onto something.'

'It's all a bit tenuous.'

'Tenuous,' said Rocco, congenially slurred, 'isn't that a bit too much of a Commissario sort of word for present company?'

'Tell us just the same,' said Assunta. 'Tenuous or distenuous.'

'It's complicated, too,' said Peroni.

'You know what he's up to?' said Rocco, turning to Assunta. 'In the old days when he was onto something good, he always used to keep quiet about it, remember? Pretended that talking would spoil it. It's the same game now.'

Through the haze of wine, it seemed to Assunta that her brother was reluctant to talk and this irritated her. 'If you ask me there's another woman in it,' she said.

'Nothing more probable.'

'Come on, Achille – talk!'

'We're not good enough for him, Assunta – couple of drunken *scugnizzi* while he's a key establishment figure – the Tyrone Power of the Italian police!'

'Rudolph Valentino, if you don't mind,' said Peroni. 'All right, I'll tell you if you insist, but don't blame me if you find it vague, complicated and inconclusive. I suppose it started because I just didn't believe that Signora Guidi had shot Lorenzo Florio-Levi, so I thought I'd try and find out. . . .'

'. . . . so I thought I'd try and find out if there were something less immediately obvious in his life for which he might have been killed.'

With the dramatic rediscovery of the old links between them, Peroni was ashamed of his reluctance to confide. The fact was that he was terrified of letting slip a clue about the truth of that other woman whose presence had been flared by Assunta's unfailing instinct. He was hesitant enough about his emotions without their inevitably derisive and bawdy comments, so he told the story avoiding Jacopa's name as much as possible and keeping his tone sternly impersonal.

Then as he talked he had the curious sensation of seeing the mosaic fragments of story in his mind's eye illuminated by a display of psychedelic lighting which showed them now in one colour, now in another, sometimes as starkly illuminated as if by lightning, sometimes in little more than a glow, occasionally annihilated altogether in pitch blackness.

It was the effect of the vast quantities of wine he was continuing to drink. That, and maybe his hand as well. Assunta had been right – he should have gone to hospital.

And yet he didn't really care one way or the other. He was too absorbed in the psychedelic spectacle in his head with its pieces of mosaic shifting kaleidoscopically as he talked. They kept forming into patterns, but never quite the right one. And yet he felt that if the lights went on for long enough, the pattern would come. Like an infinite number of monkeys with an infinite number of typewriters arriving at the *Divine Comedy*.

'. . . . where I found the two addresses which you'd given him. The first one – the house of Jacopa whatever her name is – is lived in by a very beautiful but classy sort of geisha.'

'Aha!' said Assunta. 'What did I say?'

Relieved at the equivocation, Peroni did his best to look

114

suitably confused. 'Do you know anything about her?' he asked Rocco.

'Believe it or not, I've only been in touch with her officially, over the house. I've heard tell that she's the mistress of a wealthy businessman who pays her irregularly intermittent visits.'

That squared very well, thought Peroni. 'Anyway,' he said, 'after her I went onto the second address – the home of the eccentric Englishwoman. From her I learned. . . .'

Among other things that a mystery is something dark in itself which sheds light on everything around it. His voice continuing on automatic control, Peroni found himself concentrating on that single concept. It was from that dark thing, it seemed to him, that the psychedelic lights were emanating.

'. . . . that a young German was murdered in the tower of the lesser rock. . . .'

A small part of Peroni's mind was carefully editing his account of events, and he realised that he had cut the visit to the robber's den with Jacopa's fresco portrait. At the same time he became gradually aware that there was something he should recognise in the shifting mosaic patterns. He stared at them unavailingly with his mind's eye.

'. . . . which is as far as it goes,' he heard himself concluding.

'Neapolitan baroque!' said Assunta.

'What?'

'It's all a lot of Neapolitan baroque – and that out-baroques any other baroque in the world.'

'I warned you it was complicated and inconclusive,' said Peroni, offended.

'But you didn't say it was baroque. You've always had a tendency in that direction, Achille. Sparingly applied, it's your strong point, but here it's got right out of hand. Signora Guidi and the geisha must have gone to your head.'

'You underrate Achille's instinct, Assunta,' said Rocco.

'Achille's instinct! The pair of you always did treat it as a sort of superior version of papal infallibility. The famous woman's instinct isn't even in the same league!'

'You're jealous of it, Assunta.'

'Jealous!'

115

Listening to the bickering, Peroni remembered how Rocco had always used to defend him from Assunta's onslaughts, deviating the whole discussion into a semi-amorous pecking match between the two of them. But only a small part of his attention was on their exchanges. The rest was concentrated on the psychedelically-lit patterns, trying to work out what he should be recognising in them.

Then suddenly it was illuminated in a freakish yellow flare, and to his surprise Peroni saw that it was not an answer, but a question. Or more exactly two questions.

'Excuse me a minute,' he said, 'I must telephone.' And before they could protest or question him he had gone.

He dialled Dame Iolanthe's number, and she answered at once. 'You sound as though you've been on the binge,' she said.

'I have.'

'There's a sensible man. What can I do for you?'

Peroni told her.

'I never went that far,' she said. 'And even assuming it was possible, what good could it do?'

'It could tell me why Corrado and Lorenzo were killed.'

A loud whistle nearly split Peroni's eardrum and was followed by the sound of Dame Iolanthe humming tunelessly over the line. 'Tell you what,' she said eventually, 'you might ask old Prince Frangipani – the chappie I told you about who lives in the *palazzo* in Rome where I went to the auction. He's deep into all that sort of thing.'

'Is he indeed? I'll telephone him at once.'

This was greeted by one of the Dame's fruitier chuckles. 'Afraid that's no good,' she said. 'He's a bit of a recluse – hasn't got a telephone. Your only chance is to go there.'

And then Peroni remembered that Raffaella Bonato had told him at their first encounter how Lorenzo had also gone to Rome, and she had described him as 'elated, as though he were onto the final clue in a treasure hunt.' It fitted. He looked at his watch. It was already after five. If all went smoothly, he might just get there and back by night. 'Can you give me the address?' he asked.

She dictated it to him. 'There's one of those old hand-pull bells,' she said, 'and don't be discouraged if nobody answers for twenty minutes or so. He has a long way to go, and due to his condition he walks slowly.'

Peroni thanked her and put down the receiver. If this didn't lead to the answer, probably nothing else ever would.

Scratch a Neapolitan

While he was waiting for the hire-car to arrive, Peroni telephoned the Florio-Levi works and Signorina Raffaella's pleasantly efficient voice answered.

'Something's cropped up,' he said, 'I've got to go away this evening. D'you mind if we put off our meeting till tomorrow?'

'No, that's perfectly all right,' she said, and he suspected that she sounded relieved, 'But —'

'I'll call you in the morning then.'

'Yes, but there's something else. A policeman was here this morning asking questions about you.'

'Oh.'

'He asked me to describe the man, purporting to be a policeman, who was making independent enquiries about the murder. I put him off as best I could. I gave him a very bad description of you.'

'That was kind.'

'He questioned Signorina Florio-Levi, too. I don't think he will have got much out of her, but he also asked the people in the works, and they had no reason not to say all they knew.'

'I see.'

'It's none of my business, but – be careful.'

'I'll do my best. And thank you for giving him a bad description.'

'You're welcome.'

'*Buona sera, Signorina.*'

'*Buona sera.*'

As Peroni put the receiver back, he felt a sudden nausea and spinning of the head so that he had to lean against the wall of the kiosk. But it passed, and when he came out they told him that the

117

car was ready. He climbed in and started to drive.

Although by no means in the same category as Dame Iolanthe's Bof, this hired Ritmo had a personality of its own, and a personality, moreover, incompatible with that of Peroni. The gears tended either to slip or block altogether, the mirrors swivelled alarmingly of their own accord, the driver's seat seemed bent on compressing Peroni against the steering wheel.

As he wrestled with this vehicle, Peroni tried to assess – as objectively as his almost certainly feverish state would allow – the implications of the news Signorina Raffaella had just given him. How could the police have come to learn that he was enquiring about the Florio-Levi murder? Obviously somebody who knew had told them. It was tempting to think they had done so because he was on the right track, but the evidence available didn't warrant such a conclusion. What were the chances of the police tracing him? At the moment, with a muddled description and presumably no direct line onto Rosalba or Dame Iolanthe, reasonably low. But the longer he stayed around, the more they would increase. The wisest course, sentenced the Commissario, Peroni's stern inner mentor, was to get back to Venice as soon as possible. Once reinstated there it should be no problem dealing with any possible consequences the irresponsible escapade might have. He would be entrenched and official once more.

In Assisi, the sound-headed functionary went on, he had a lot to lose and nothing to gain. Assunta was right: what he was doing was dangerous. If it came out that a policeman in his position had been setting up an enquiry in competition with the official one, a lot of people would snatch at the opportunity as a stick to beat him with. It was just the sort of impropriety which, stained with political colouring, as such things always were in Italy, would be sufficient to ruin a career.

The only sensible thing was to back out fast, abandoning for a start the present mission which was an archetypal wild-goose chase and could only involve him more deeply.

And quite apart from the quixotic nature of it, the physical danger involved in the journey should be enough to make cancellation a necessity. Light headed and feverish, with an infected hand, he was in no condition to make a long night drive.

118

And, as if that wasn't enough, he was still awash with the incalculable amount of wine he had consumed with Rocco and Assunta. To drive in that state was tantamount to suicide.

With a bad grace, the steering wheel tugging against him, the Ritmo turned into the approach road to the autostrada.

And Assunta's jibe about Neapolitan baroque was richly deserved. He was creating nothing but unnecessary and fantastic complications. How could events in the thirteenth century influence twentieth century lives? The lovers' tiff solution was infinitely more feasible.

At this point, the sensible reasoning was interrupted by a sybilline inner whisper which he recognised with surprise and some misgiving as that of the *scugnizzo*, the Commissario's eternal scourge. But, said the whisper, when all's said and done Lorenzo was in search of something, Corrado was killed for something. Those things happened, and you're not going to be happy until you find out why.

At the price of health, career, sanity, maybe life itself? snapped back the Commissario. Let's not be absurd. The thing has gone too far already. You can live a perfectly fulfilled life without prying into something that happened in thirteenth century Assisi.

It was beginning to get dark. The red and green lights of the autostrada check-in shone brightly ahead of him. Turn back before it's too late, insisted the Commissario urgently. You passed a motel a couple of kilometres back. Go back there, have your hand seen to, spend the night there and call Assunta to join you and drive back to Verona tomorrow morning. It's the only sane course.

And Jacopa? whispered the *scugnizzo*, would you abandon her, too?

That is the greatest absurdity of all! erupted the Commissario, and you were the first to say so. There is no Jacopa to abandon. She has been in a tomb for more than seven centuries. Go back to the motel and sanity.

For once the Commissario was indisputably right. To continue with things as they now stood was pure lunacy. Coming up to the check-in, Peroni yanked at the steering wheel to make a U-turn.

The fact that he didn't make one, he never knew whether to

ascribe to his own semi-delirious state, to the cantankerous personality of the Ritmo or to some perverse intervention of the *scugnizzo*. But before he had time to reopen negotiations he had taken a ticket and allowed the Ritmo to head in the direction of Rome.

'Speaking as a Neapolitan rather than as a Superintendent of Fine Arts, this is the building where I feel most at home.'

Assunta looked at the temple before which they were standing with its six high columns supporting the roof of the pronaos. 'It's – uncharacteristic,' she said, feeling the observation was a stupid one.

'Exactly,' said Rocco, 'Because it's pagan. Inside there's a Christian church, but they never succeeded in destroying the pagan spirit of the place. Not for nothing is it still called the temple of Minerva. And that's why I feel at home here. I think most Neapolitans remain pagan beneath a veneer of Christianity. Certainly I do. And so, I feel fairly sure, do you and Achille.'

Assunta looked at him standing beside her and thought that his high, ugly, scored face reminded her of a pagan god. Suddenly she felt scared. Maybe he was right, and she was essentially pagan, too, and all the carefully constructed Christianity of her life – marriage, family, mass on Sunday, confession and all the rest – was only a veneer.

Till now she had enjoyed the excitement that Rocco had aroused in her ever since the lady in the restaurant had unwittingly unleashed his true *scugnizzo* self. She had let herself go in the certainty that it was a limited, provisional adventure against·the safe, permanent background of the family in Verona, but now she was no longer sure that the background was either safe or permanent. The past, which she had romantically dreamed of re-finding as a brief escape from housework and children, had suddenly materialised and was threatening to snatch her away for ever into the endless glades of a pagan wood.

'You haven't told me about your marriage,' said Rocco as they mounted the half dozen steps that led up between the columns into the pronaos.

'There's not a lot to tell,' she said, trying to keep her voice

120

normal. 'After a certain number of years most happy marriages are much the same.'

'It's happy then?'

'Oh yes.' She tried to sound serene and not defiant about it.

'So tell me.'

She started to talk about Giorgio and their relationship and the children, feeling half ashamed of how poor and ordinary it all sounded.

'I don't call that happiness,' said Rocco when she had finished, 'I call it resignation.'

'What about your marriage?' she said, avoiding the issue.

'It's hell on earth,' said Rocco. 'Veronica is a neurotic, jealous bitch. We have a large house in the hills towards Gualdo Tadino, and there's not a square centimetre of it where I can call my soul my own.'

Assunta felt a surge of unholy exhilaration. 'Why don't you leave her then?'

'Because she's rich.'

'You never did mince words, did you?'

After the bright May sunlight outside it seemed almost dark within the pronaos. Assunta stood with her back against the wall in one corner and Rocco stood in front of her, leaning with one hand on the stone behind her. This is how young lovers stand together, she thought.

'What's the point? I knew too well and for too long what it's like to be poor, and now that I've got a source of money I don't intend to abandon it.'

Far from repelling her, she found this ruthlessness attractive. Other men would have glossed over the calculation; Rocco flaunted it, and she counted it for virility in him.

'Not even if you fell in love with somebody else?' She didn't know herself whether the question was out before she had time to monitor it or whether she had connived at its escape.

'It would depend on how much I loved her.'

For the first time in more years than she could count, Assunta knew she was attractive. This attraction, which she thought had been long doused by drudgery and strident, combative mother-hood, seemed to be exuding from her body like an exotic sweat, and she knew very well the effect it was having on Rocco. It gave her a sense of power.

His other hand was on the stone behind her now, so that she was caged by his arms, and his ugly-lovely face, giving off a not unattractive whiff of grappa, was moving towards hers. She felt herself being impelled through the back gates of Minerva's temple towards the endless glades.

And then, ignorant of the process that made her do so, she pushed herself free of him.

'Not now, Rocco – not yet anyway. I can't throw away a life on the spur of the moment. Not when I'm three quarters drunk. Let me go back to the hotel – I want to sober up.'

Rocco looked at her, the lines shifting enigmatically, finally resolving into a crooked smile. 'OK,' he said, 'I won't try to force you. But can I take you out tomorrow morning? Let me show you round. Assisi on May Day's a sight not to be missed. A surprisingly pagan sight.'

'I'd like that.'

He took her arm, and they walked away from the endless glades and back into Assisi, but Assunta knew she would be waiting for him tomorrow like a girl in love for the first time.

Violent Death – Ancient and Modern

Peroni saw at once what Dame Iolanthe had meant about Prince Frangipani's condition. The old man was bent almost entirely double so that his voice now came from a point more or less level with Peroni's navel.

'A Commissario of Police, you say? I am delighted to make your acquaintance.'

His hand came up to shake Peroni's, and ridiculous though the gesture should have looked coming from that hoop of a body, there was something exquisitely courteous about it, as though he were receiving a guest of particular honour.

'Come along in, won't you? I'm afraid the place is a bit of a mess.'

Peroni wondered briefly at the absence of surprise with which the old Prince had accepted the fact that his nocturnal visitor was a policeman. But then, stepping inside the massive door, his attention was at once taken up with his surroundings. The great hall with its furniture wrapped in sheets was chilly in spite of the warm Roman evening outside and lit only by a flickering lantern which the Prince was holding. In Peroni's semi-delirious state the weirdness of it all seemed quite natural.

'Shall I lead the way? I must apologise for the absence of electrical lighting. When I was left alone here I had it cut off. It hurt my eyes.'

As they started to climb a dusty spiral stairway Peroni was again struck by the old man's extraordinary courtesy. It wasn't the guarded congeniality of most encounters, nor was it even just good manners; it was a sort of spontaneous reverence for a dignity which, until then, Peroni had never even dreamed that he might possess.

And then with a shock he realised that the Prince was a descendant of Jacopa, and that must have been how she behaved, too. Ridiculous, of course, to stretch the link too far; with all the time that had intervened there must have been enough genetic mutations to render almost any European alive as much a descendant of Jacopa as was the Prince. Still, it was the same family.

'I'm afraid we have rather a lot of ground to cover. When I made an apartment for myself in the remotest corner of what was formerly the servants' quarters, it was generally held to be an old man's perverseness – though some employed stronger terms. In point of fact, it's the most comfortable part of the building.'

The shadow of his almost circular frame, followed by that of Peroni, was thrown about by the lantern-light from wall to wall, down corridors and up stairs, and even occasionally tossed up towards the high ceilings as though they were playing an elaborate and independent game of tag.

In Peroni's mind, flickering as alarmingly as the lantern-light, it seemed as though this journey through the abandoned palace would go on for ever, but eventually the Prince stopped outside a door in a linoleum-covered stone corridor.

123

'My living space,' he announced, opening the door. 'Somewhat limited, but considerably more ample than the coffin which will be my next lodging.'

It was indeed small and of monastic simplicity. A bed with a bare wooden cross at its head, a wooden table, one or two chairs, a rudimentary desk and a large book-case, but the candle and lamp lighting gave Peroni the sense of stumbling across a border into fairyland.

'Please be seated,' said the Prince, 'I hope you'll forgive the spartan quality of the furniture. Perhaps you will allow me to mitigate it with a glass of Frascati.'

Peroni allowed him.

'This wine,' said the Prince, pouring two glasses, 'is the only luxury I am able to retain. The family vineyards, alas, have passed into other hands, but the peasants still kindly keep me supplied.'

His head still ineluctably pressed floorwards, the Prince raised his glass towards Peroni's in an elegantly formal gesture of salute. They drank. Peroni was never to know afterwards whether it was due to his own inflamed imbalance or not, but it seemed to him as though the wine had an almost unearthly flavour such as no Frascati he had ever tasted before.

'I am,' said the Prince, after they had savoured the wine in silence for a few seconds, 'at your complete disposition.'

'If you'll forgive the observation,' said Peroni, 'you don't seem in the least curious about a policeman calling on you at such an hour.'

'I presumed you would explain matters when it seemed proper to you.'

One does not ask people to give an account of themselves, the gently courteous voice seemed to imply.

'Perhaps I can best do so,' said Peroni, 'with another question. Does the name Lorenzo Florio-Levi mean anything to you?'

It was a handicap not to be able to see the Prince's face because all those reactions which only the eyes reveal went unobserved, but the voice when it came seemed as unperturbably detached as before.

'Indeed it does. He came to see me about a fortnight ago.'

124

'*Buona notte, papa.*'

Raffaella bent over and kissed her father on the forehead. As always when her regular Friday night visits drew to a close she felt herself torn. She was longing to get into the fresh air, away from the stuffy, claustrophobic room with its hundreds of old family photographs and worthless bric-a-brac that were for him the memories of a lifetime. But she also experienced remorse and regret at the prospect of leaving him. He was completely alone and, apart from a woman who came in to tidy up, Raffaella's visits were all he had. Besides, each was now the other's only remaining close relative, and if there wasn't a great deal of communication between them, there was genuine fondness.

'You'd better be careful, Raffaella,' he said.

'Careful? Whatever for?'

'If what you told me is true. . . .'

'Oh, don't worry about that, papa! I'm perfectly safe.'

'You want to be careful just the same.'

She glanced at the heavy clock to which she used to confide secrets when she was a little girl. '*Santo cielo!*' she said, 'I really must go, papa – it's nearly midnight and I've got to walk home and be ready in the office by eight o'clock in the morning.' She gave him another kiss. 'Call me if there's anything you want, and I'll be back for supper next Friday. *Ciao, papa!*'

'*Ciao*, Raffaella.'

As always at these partings he raised his hand in a little gesture which might have been salutation or an incoherent attempt to call her back, and she broke quickly away to escape the guilty feeling that she ought to try and find out which.

Her father's apartment was in a building identical to many others standing in rows along a series of rising terraces. The authorities of Assisi, who guard their medieval patrimony with ruthless zeal, would have looked more favourably on mass murder than on modern building anywhere near the city. But people need houses to live in, so this functional, undistinguished suburb of Assisi stands discreetly out of sight round the corner of Mount Subasio, cheerfully heedless of history.

Raffaella turned round by the back of her father's house and started to climb down one of the many flights of steps which linked one terrace to another. It was a warm, starry night, and she was glad of the twenty minutes' walk to her own apartment in Assisi itself as a pause in which to try and sort things out.

Reaching the bottom of the steps, she turned into one of the small streets which run through the suburb.

She was much absorbed in her own thoughts and didn't notice the sound of a car engine being turned on some way down the street behind her.

Peroni felt a catch of excitement. He had been more than half expecting that he was on the right path, but confirmation of it had all the effect of a sudden glint of gold in the dug earth.

'Did you know,' Peroni continued, 'that he was killed last Tuesday?'

'Killed? Poor young fellow! How very shocking!' Once again a glimpse of the Prince's face would have been invaluable to decide whether he was taken as totally unawares as his words indicated, but the tone of shock sounded genuine. 'Indeed, I knew nothing of it. How did it happen?'

'He was shot. May I ask you what he came to see you about?'

'He said he was writing his graduate thesis and for this he was seeking information about two members of my family in the thirteenth century.'

Another glint of gold.

'Two you say? And who were they?'

'The sons of a certain Jacopa de Settesoli.'

Now a fair-sized chunk of gold had been exposed.

'Were you able to tell him anything?'

'I was able to give him some information, yes. Necessarily it was scrappy; it is hard to piece together a coherent account of people's lives when they were lived so long ago, but I take a keen interest in such matters, and circumstances were unusually propitious as my family has always been accustomed to keeping records, so a mass of material is available. From this I was able to gather some material to answer his question.'

'Would you mind telling me what you told him?'

'By all means. Perhaps we might refill our glasses first?' Peroni

126

raised no objection to this proposal. 'This Jacopa de Settesoli had two sons,' the Prince went on, 'The elder, Giovanni, embarked on a military career and was renowned for his exceptional valour and generosity.'

Peroni remembered Jacopa's first letter to her sons in which she mentioned Giovanni's tendency to throw himself headlong into adventure – 'a trait that goes hand in hand with courage and generosity'.

'He fought in many campaigns and in 1248 he sailed for the crusades once again, with Louis IX this time, and while marching on Cairo he was killed in an unexpected and ferocious Saracen attack.' There was a pause and the rounded body seemed to twitch with a sudden spasm of pain. 'As for Graziano,' the old man continued, 'he had an altogether less honourable career terminating in a dishonourable death.'

('I hope that you, Graziano, are correcting your vision of the world as a private orchard in which all the juiciest apples belong to you.')

'He ran away from the family home before he was out of his teens and never returned. There are various legends concerning his activities. He is said to have been both mercenary and bandit and, in a violent age, was notorious for his violence. The strange story of his death, however, is a documented fact, though what lay behind it has never been explained and now almost certainly never will be. Some time after the death of his mother in Assisi he arrived in the city with a small group of ruffians which he appears to have recruited himself. He was surprised with them by night making an armed raid on the New Church.'

Peroni's mind snapped with sudden tension. The New Church was the one Signora Guidi had evinced such unusual interest in.

'They put up a most violent resistance,' the Prince went on, 'and there was what amounted to pitched battle in Assisi. Graziano and, so far as we know, his companions were killed during the course of it. That is as much as we know.'

But quite enough, thought Peroni excitedly. 'What was Lorenzo's reaction to this story?' he asked.

'A most surprising exhilaration. I remember thinking at the time that it seemed out of proportion to the mere discovery of material for a thesis.' There was a sudden tension in the hoop-shaped body. 'But surely, my dear Commissario, you're not suggesting that there is some sort of connection between what I have been telling you and the death of the wretched young man who came to see me two weeks ago?'

'I think that now that's just exactly what I am suggesting,' said Peroni.

The light shed by the darkness of the mystery was growing brighter.

As Raffaella walked along the street she thought about the unusual and really very good looking policeman who had presented himself under false pretences. In her position she should have taken a stronger line over that. And was he even a policeman at all? If his first story had been false, then why not his second as well? And yet what motive could he have for lying? And besides, she trusted him instinctively, which was more than she could say for the indisputably genuine one.

She was unaware of the car which was now coming slowly up the street behind her.

Did she really trust him, though, or did she rather feel a dangerous weakness for him which was quite another thing? And if she really did trust him, then why had she not told him the full story about the keys? Because, she answered herself, a policeman is always a policeman. If she had revealed to him what was, after all, no more than a suspicion, however appalling, there was no telling what use he might have made of the information. He could have ruined everything.

Raffaella walked out into the winding main road that went down to the medieval city. She didn't see the car which had stopped at the end of the street she had just emerged from.

But he wasn't the sort to ruin everything. A man who could put his own career at risk in order to pursue what he believed was the truth was a man to be trusted. It would have been better to have told him and asked his advice rather than take the course she had done.

Raffaella continued to walk down the deserted road which was dark, with the suburb lights now out of sight round the bend and the lights of Assisi proper still not in sight. She neither saw nor heard the car pulling out into the main road behind her.

Her father's fears were unjustified, of course. There could be no danger. Nevertheless, what she had done was imprudent.

She started to cross the road.

If the good-looking policeman had come that evening as planned, she would have told him. He would have relieved her of the weight of being the only one to know, and by now she would have had nothing to worry about. Tomorrow then. He had said he would call her tomorrow, and when he did she would tell him everything. The decision eased her mind considerably.

The car was upon her before she had time to react. She had the impression of a black mass of hostile matter avalanching towards her. Even in her terror, as she started to run, she wondered why the headlights had been switched off. Then the car, swerving slightly, struck her full on. She had never felt anything like even a millionth part of the violence of the impact; it was as though the world had exploded. She felt herself hurtling through the air for an impossibly long time, then crashing into the ground with another impact of unimaginable violence which smashed out everything but a protesting flicker of consciousness.

Then the horror crushed her head and even the flicker was gone.

At the Gate of the Winds

It seemed as though the Middle Ages had taken over altogether. Everywhere you looked there were flag-bearers, minstrels, jugglers, crossbowmen, drummers and other musicians dressed in many-coloured jerkins and tights. Dazzlingly variegated flags whirled through the air in displays of virtuosity or hung from walls and buildings and shops. The bars, re-converted to taverns, were crowded beyond all verisimilitude. Assisi was plunged in riotous and pagan adoration of the newly-arrived spring.

On his arrival back there, Peroni was momentarily taken aback by this unbridled outburst of medievalism, for he had forgotten

129

all about its being May Day. But once he had got the costumed frenzy placed, he forgot about it except for its nuisance value as something to be fought through in order to get at something else. The New Church.

As soon as he had learnt of Graziano's mysterious assault and death, he had been convinced that the end of his real pilgrimage lay here. Lorenzo, of course, had been ahead of him, but whatever material object might be at the end of the trail (assuming there was one) and even if Lorenzo had removed it, the building itself or somebody connected with it must provide the answer.

His first impulse on leaving Prince Frangipani had been to drive straight back to Assisi, but then he realised that this would be not only stupid but also pointless as the church would be closed. Instead he got himself a pizza and went back to the Ritmo with the intention of getting an hour's sleep in it before starting the journey back. But in fact it was already dawn when he awoke, pleasantly surprised to find himself refreshed, vigorous and with his hand apparently back to normal.

He drove the strangely compliant Ritmo back to Assisi, and by the time he got there the May Day festivities were already in full swing. Then, having returned the car to the hire firm and enquired the whereabouts of the New Church, he started to fight his way there through the crowd.

The church was central, so even against the heavy odds it only took him a few minutes to get there, but when he reached the little square in front of it he halted, staring in bewildered horror as his entire intricate edifice of deduction collapsed in a heap of rubble. For the New Church was exactly what its name said it was – new. It must have been about seventeenth century and, with fitting irony, its style was baroque.

His hopes revived briefly when he went inside and found that it was built on the remains of St Francis's birthplace, parts of which could be visited. But the revival was a brief one, for although some building on that spot did span the seven hundred years, it was not the New Church.

Wrapped in thunder-cloud depression, he left the building and made his way unseeingly through the brilliant crowd. After walking for an uncalculated time, he found himself at a spot he remembered from the first day. It was a stone archway up a slope beside the cathedral of San Rufino, and it was known, don Sereno had said, as the gate of the winds. In fact, even on such a mild morning as this a wind was blowing in through it from Mount Subasio.

He looked up at a brightly-coloured plaque on the wall with a quote from St Francis's Canticle of All Created Things. 'Praised be, my Lord, for brother wind and for the air, cloudy and fair and in all weathers by which you give sustenance to your creatures.' He felt absurdly as though the medieval Italian words were tugging him back across the centuries to a time long before the New Church was built.

Then, as he looked down from the plaque, he saw a group of costumed people coming in through the gate, several of them on horseback, and he had to stand back to let them pass.

This group was headed by a richly dressed man in his fifties with a lean, intelligent face, clamped mouth and eyes which looked as though he were watching for an assassin. Immediately to his right rode a handsome, tough-looking young man with blonde hair. The two of them sounded a little chime of recognition in Peroni's mind, though he didn't immediately realise why. Then it came to him. The men neatly fitted his mental image of the Venetian ambassador, Morosino, and his young German lover, Corrado di Turingia.

Come to think of it the embassy which arrived in Assisi from Venice at exactly the same time of year in 1230 must have been very similar to this present group. There were about half a dozen principal members while outriders and guards could be seen through the gateway.

As Peroni watched, the riders came to a halt, and the man who could have been Morosino swung off his horse and walked forward to shake hands with a small, fat man who squinnied welcome with piggy eyes.

Suddenly Peroni felt badly scared. Maybe his hand wasn't back to normal after all and the past was ambushing him in his delirium. No doubt, the fat man *could* have been messer Ugo da Palazzo greeting the Venetian ambassador.

He knew his only chance was to break the link by getting away, but he felt physically incapable of moving. He continued to stare – fascinated, appalled, terrified, absorbed – at the group of riders. One of them, a good-looking young man with an intelligent, half mocking expression, was taking advantage of the halt to speak with someone who must have been standing near the gate, though Peroni could not see this person for the press of horses and people.

He moved in order to be able to look from a different angle and then, when he had succeeded in doing so, he felt all his previous emotions engulfed in a giant wave of incredulous delight. The person the young man was talking to was a woman in medieval costume. She was wearing the same russet dress as the woman he had glimpsed on his arrival in Assisi and her face, beyond all doubt, was the face of the woman in the fresco.

She was listening, joy in repose, to what the young man was saying, occasionally nodding. It looked as though they were making some sort of appointment.

Then the totally unexpected happened. She lifted her eyes, dark chestnut, and looked across the street at Peroni. She gave no other sign, but for what felt like a long time she perceived him, taking in his existence; and he, in the same way, knew her. If they had been lovers the intimacy could not have been closer. Finally she lowered her eyes again and it was as though she were slowly (reluctantly?) withdrawing into her own time.

Now he no longer cared whether plunges into the past were dangerous or not. Pushing and dodging his way among horses and people (Was he the only person in modern clothes? Could the others see him? The questions flicked through his mind as he went, but he gave them no importance) he made his way across the road.

He was more than half expecting her not to be there, but she was, her face turned away from him as she listened to the man.

At that moment, the leader of the group having climbed back onto his horse, the whole party started to ride on, and the good-looking man raised his hand in salute as he rejoined them. As soon as he was out of the way, Peroni accosted the woman.

'*Mi scusi. . . .*' he said. It wasn't particularly original, but originality needed time.

'*Si?*' She turned to look at him, unsurprised and enquiring, and Peroni stared wildly at her. There was a certain similarity of features, but she was not the same woman, and there was no trace of recognition in her eyes.

'I'm sorry,' said Peroni, noticing with alarm that he was floundering, 'I thought we'd met somewhere before. I'm very sorry. . . .'

'Not at all.'

Her smile seemed to imply that even if they hadn't met before, she would have no objections to doing so now, but Peroni was in no mood to take the hint.

The Mortification of Commissario Zanetti

'Are the two killings linked?'

That was the question Commissario Zanetti had been dreading ever since he had heard that Raffaella Bonato had been killed by a hit-and-run driver the previous evening. It was a reasonable inference that the two deaths were linked, but if they were it was most improbable that Signora Guidi had been responsible for the first one, and the thought that he might have been wrong about that galled Zanetti as much as a major election trouncing for the Party.

And the fact that the question – put during the morning conference at the *Questura* in Perugia – should have been asked by the Perugia police chief made it incomparably more galling. For the Perugia police chief was a fascist. Not just a generical fascist like anybody who wasn't a Communist, but a card-holding member of the Movimento Sociale Italiano, the heir and direct descendant of Mussolini's fascist party.

'It's a possibility,' Zanetti admitted reluctantly.

But still only a possibility, he consoled himself. His first theory was that it had been no more than the hit-and-run accident it appeared to be, but the total absence of brake-marks made this unlikely, and he had had to abandon the position altogether when the killer car had been found abandoned in a clump of trees only a few minutes' drive away, and it transpired that it had been stolen the night before from a surveyor in Assisi who, it now seemed practically certain, had no connection with Raffaella Bonato or the Florio-Levis and who had flawless alibis for both murders.

'You don't sound very convinced?' The police chief's tone was suave as always when he was at his most perfidious.

'I don't want to jump to conclusions, *dottore*,' said Zanetti righteously. 'The only certain link is her place of employment, and the two types of killing are completely different.'

'Have you any other suggestion, *dottore*?'

'The death of Signorina Bonato,' said Zanetti, 'has all the marks of a Mafia or Camorra killing.'

As he knew it would, that gave pause to the police chief. The ruthless mowing down of a 'traitor' by car did look very like the Mafia or the Camorra.

'Is there anything to indicate that she might have been involved with either of them?'

'No, but until now there has been nothing to orient our enquiries in that direction.'

'And has there been anything to orient your enquiries toward *any* possible motive for the killing of Signorina Bonato?'

Badly nettled, Zanetti tried to retain political objectivity. 'Nothing specific,' he said. But the police chief remained silent, emphasising the inadequacy of the reply, and forcing Zanetti to continue against his strategical better judgement. 'If Florio-Levi was not killed by the Guidi woman then presumably Signorina Bonato's death occurred within the same circumstantial context as his.'

'Ah!' It was a mere exhalation of breath, but the satisfaction it conveyed suggested that Zanetti's admission was tantamount to a renegation on the policy of state control of industry. 'I suppose,' went on the police chief, pursuing his advantage with smooth ruthlessness, 'that we have no idea what that circumstantial context might be?'

'No, *dottore*.'

'Well then,' the police chief pursued amiably, 'for one thing we will treat the two deaths as a joint enquiry, provisionally at any rate, and for another I want an exhaustive enquiry into the general backgrounds of both Florio-Levi and Raffaella Bonato.'

'*Si, dottore.*'

'By the way, what was she doing on that road at that time of night?'

Zanetti felt a lift of relief that here at least he was one step ahead of the reactionaries. 'She had spent the evening with her father,' he said. 'Apparently it was her custom to walk out to have supper with him at his home in the new Assisi housing area.'

'So somebody who knew her habits could have followed her and waited for her to come out?'

'*Si, dottore.*'

'Have you seen the father?'

'I haven't had time. I'll be visiting him as soon as this conference terminates.'

'Yes, well I think that just about determines the course of action for the immediate future. We'll meet again to discuss the Assisi deaths this afternoon.' He seemed to glance with satisfaction at the political carnage he had caused, then went on, 'Oh, there's just one more thing. What about this man who's been falsely representing himself as a policeman?'

Scansani shifted unhappily; he didn't like speaking in front of an audience. 'My enquiries aren't yet finished,' he said. 'So far I've only succeeded in questioning people at the Florio-Levi works, and there is a certain – disparity in the description of the man which they gave me. The workmen described him as southern looking, whereas Signorina Bonato said he had a marked northern appearance. And Signorina Florio-Levi said —'
He paused, apparently hesitant as to whether he should even refer her impression.

'Well?' prompted the police chief.

'She said,' went on Scansani unwillingly, 'that he looked like an archangel.'

Eyebrows soared all round the table.

The police chief drummed his fingers on the table in what looked to Zanetti like a provocative right-wing manner. 'If there is one thing,' he said at last, 'which is unequivocal in the Italian consciousness, it is the distinction between north and south, so, leaving aside theological considerations, that particular disparity seems to me indicative.' He paused, fascistically hyena-ish. 'It is beginning to look as though the tracing of this man is becoming one of our top priorities.'

'Still in search of Jacopa, Commissario?'

It was perhaps the only voice which could have penetrated the clouds of bewilderment and shock in which Peroni's mind had been wrapped since his experience at the gate of the winds. Turning, he saw Dame Iolanthe bearing down on him like a consort battleship. Her figure was rendered even more impressive than usual by the fact that she was in full medieval attire with a purple embroidered dress stretching magnificently behind her and a wimple almost as large as the cabin of a railway engine. This dramatic temporary concession to femininity so dominated the scene that it was only after Peroni had been looking for a couple of seconds that he realised Alice was there, too, swathed in the same drifting, hesitant stuffs as she had worn at their first meeting.

'What a pleasant surprise,' he said, meaning it.

'Let's go and have a bottle of wine. I know a pretty decent little pub just round the corner.'

'Iolanthe, don't you think a cup of tea —'

'Stuff and nonsense, Alice! Can't you get the disgusting stuff out of your head? The effect it has on the human stomach is quite indescribable. Edgar Wallace died of it, you know. And I knew a stage-door keeper in London, a hopeless tea addict, whose kidneys. . . .'

With the Dame rattling anecdotally on, they set off for her pub. As they were walking, Peroni noticed a couple of lovers coming towards them and realised with a shock that they were his sister and Rocco. They were so absorbed in each other that they passed within centimetres without being aware of him. In spite of his own emotional turmoil, Peroni felt a brief shrill of alarm at the situation. A passing flirtation was one thing, a passionate romance was another.

'Here we are then,' Dame Iolanthe's voice postponed his anxiety.

Her pub was so crowded that you had the impression people were jostling about all the way up to the ceiling, but such was the force of the Dame's personality, not to mention her shoulders and voice, that the three of them were quickly seated at a table with a bottle of wine and a small pot of camomile for Alice.

'Well, Commissario, you haven't answered my question.'

'What question was that?'

'Are you still looking for Jacopa?'

'As a matter of fact, I thought I saw her a few minutes ago.'

The need to communicate was urgent, but the whole thing was so wild and improbable that he spoke in a light, conversational tone in order that it could be received as a piece of banter. He was therefore the more surprised when she took him completely seriously.

'You did?' she said, then lifting her glass, 'Cheers! Tell me about it.'

'Oh, of course it wasn't her really. But just for a second I thought. . . .' Fumblingly he tried to describe the experience. 'Then when I went up to her,' he concluded, 'it turned out to be just another young woman in medieval dress.'

'You're quiet sure of that?'

'What do you mean?'

'Oh, don't get me wrong, Commissario. I don't believe in spiritualism or anything like that – lot of damn rubbish if you ask me, phosphorescent jelly fish floating through the air and grasping old harridans with devices fitted between their thighs. But I do believe in the tricks that time can play. You remember Einstein and all that stuff about trains rushing through space and immobile observers watching them? What I mean is that time, in a sense, is an artificial element created for us to live in as an aquarium is for fish because in our present form we couldn't exist in timelessness. But just because it's artificial there can be flaws in it, it can become rucked up so to speak so that people at altogether different points of its sequence meet until it's smoothed out again.'

'But who does the rucking up?' asked Peroni.

The Dame looked at him shrewdly. 'Could be anybody,' she said. 'In this case it could be Jacopa herself. It could even be you.'

'Me?' said Peroni startled.

'Why not? You don't have to have read Einstein to be able to ruck up time. You can do it without even realising what you're at. There are certain places, too, where it happens more easily than others. And if I had to choose one single place as particularly liable to rucks, that place would be Assisi.'

'But why?'

'My good man,' cried the Dame, knocking back an entire glass in her fervour, 'Just look about you! The past is vibrating everywhere! Indeed, to judge by some of the tourists you get here these days, the past is considerably more lively than the present.'

Peroni's wonder-loving Neapolitan soul would dearly have loved to accept the theory lock, stock and barrel, but as a rationalistic septentrionised policeman he felt obliged to reject it no less thoroughly. His mind see-sawed giddily with the conflict and reached no equilibrium.

'Apropos,' she went on, leaning back and tilting up the front legs of her chair in a manner that would have been more appropriate if she had been in her customary male attire, 'I hope we shall be seeing you on the helicopter jaunt this afternoon.'

Peroni remembered the tickets Rocco had given him and Assunta. 'I daresay,' he said.

'Capital! It's just what you need. I'm a great believer in flight for states of emotional upheaval. What you need, Commissario, is an aerial view of things.'

Mourning and Monarchy

The only celebrations that Commissario Zanetti could tolerate were the *Feste dell'Unità*, those rowdy jamborees with dancing and gastronomic stands, held up and down Italy to promote the sale of the Communist Party daily newspaper. Consequently he was relieved to be in the relative tranquillity of the new housing estate and away from the reactionary glorification of the Dark Ages being held in Assisi.

138

On the landing outside the front door of the little apartment in which Raffaella Bonato's father lived there was a little group of women with expressions compounded of awe and excitement at being even as close as this to violent death. Zanetti knew the reaction well and considered it a typically bourgeois lack of realism.

The women recognised him immediately as police and moved aside to let him pass. He rang the bell and the door was answered by another woman obviously belonging to the same category.

'*Questura*,' he said, showing her his card.

'He's mourning,' said the woman. 'Is it really necessary now?'

'I'm afraid so,' said Zanetti, thinking how strange it was that people thought exceptions could be made in official procedure to suit individual circumstances.

'He's in here.'

One glance at the old man was enough to tell Zanetti that the interview was not going to be easy. He was seated at the table staring at a large photograph of his daughter and making strange choking noises. His situation, Zanetti realised, was hardly an optimum one, but people would save themselves a lot of unnecessary suffering if only they would learn to think politically about these things.

'Your daughter was here for supper last night?' he said after presenting himself.

The old man stared at him incomprehendingly.

'Your daughter,' he tried again, enunciating with exaggerated clarity as though he were talking to an idiot, 'she was here with you last night?'

But the old man just continued to stare as though Zanetti wasn't even there.

'Signor Bonato,' said Zanetti, maintaining patience with difficulty, 'if you want the facts about your daughter's decease established you really must endeavour to collaborate.'

The old man's eyes remained as sightless and as senseless as before. Zanetti looked about in some exasperation; there seemed to be no solution to the problem.

'Is he always like this?' he asked, getting up and going to the woman who was still in the room.

'He's mourning,' she repeated, irritating Zanetti, who felt there was an emotionally non-political undertone in the word.

'I warned you.'

But it was not the woman who spoke, and the words were eerie in the silence. Turning, Zanetti saw that the old man had addressed them to his daughter's photograph.

'What do you mean?' he asked, going quickly back to the table.

'I warned you,' said the old man, still addressing the photograph, 'I told you to be careful.'

'What did you warn her? What did you tell her to be careful about?'

'You said you were perfectly safe,' he went on, apparently unaware of Zanetti's presence, 'but you weren't, were you?'

'Signor Bonato, please answer my question!'

'If you'd stayed here you'd still be alive now.'

'Signor Bonato —'

'What was it you warned your daughter?'

To his chagrin Zanetti saw that the woman, who shouldn't even have been there in the first place, was kneeling beside the old man talking in the ridiculously soothing voice, so inimical to constructive political thought, that women used with children. And what was worse, it seemed to be working; she was getting through to him.

'What did you warn your daughter?' she repeated.

'I warned her that she was in danger.'

'How was she in danger?'

He looked up at her, still apparently unaware of Zanetti's presence. 'Last night we were talking about the murder,' he said. 'I asked her why the woman had shot him, and she said, 'I don't think she did shoot him, papa – and what's more I'm very much afraid that now I know who did.'

But when, on Zanetti's urgent insistence, the woman enquired who his daughter had been referring to, the old man shook his head and replied that she had refused to say.

In the place of honour on the wall there hung a large photograph of the late Umberto of Savoy, former King of Italy, flanked by broad tricolour ribbons.

'His Late Majesty,' Amos Butturini said, in case Scansani should have overlooked the point.

The room had various mirrors and, having made his initial reverence to the monarchy, the dwarf started to observe himself in them with great frequency and delight. And where he was not able to admire himself in reflection he could do so in image, for the room was also hung thick with photographs of Amos Butturini and framed newspaper and magazine cuttings. There was Amos beaming triumphantly at the camera lens or clasped in the arms of show-biz personalities, and there were headlines such as THE MIDGET WITH THE MIGHTY MEMORY and TV'S TINY TON OF TALENT.

The interview had started out in the hall under difficult circumstances because two seemingly unstoppable dalmatians had got it into their spotted heads that Scansani was there to dismember their miniature master, and it was their evident intention to carry out the operation first on Scansani. Only after some minutes of bedlam during which the hall was a whirl of black spots and shrill cries of 'Belle! Arlette! Down this instant, Signorina!' were the dogs somehow ejected into the garden and Scansani ushered into the *salotto*.

'I'm sorry we're having to take up more of your time,' said Scansani.

'That is perfectly all right,' said Amos Butturini regally. 'In spite of my monarchical faith I believe it my duty to do everything in my power to assist the authorities, even when the country is a republic.'

'Quite so,' said Scansani for want of apter comment, 'but what I came to ask you about,' he went on, 'is whether anybody, apart from Commissario Zanetti, has tried to ask you questions, posing as a policeman.'

Amos Butturini cocked his large head like a judicious bird studying a suspect crumb. He then pursed his lips, thought for a second and finally said, 'No.'

Another wasted visit, thought Scansani.

But the dwarf's observation of the crumb was not yet finished. He continued to regard it, pursing his lips some more, and then produced a second monosyllable. 'Why?'

141

Scansani was taken aback; he was not accustomed to witnesses putting questions to him, but the dwarf's manner was so imperious that he felt impelled to answer. 'We're anxious to trace somebody who is going about posing as a policeman.'

'Description.' Definitely an imperative.

'We have no very accurate description so far,' said Scansani, feeling on the defensive. 'Several witnesses described him as southern looking and —'

'I observed a man of southern aspect in the vicinity of the Florio-Levi works on Tuesday night. He seemed to be acting in a suspicious manner, and I had the impression he was following Signora Guidi.'

If Scansani had not been sitting, he would have staggered. 'Why didn't you mention this before?' he asked.

'Because nobody asked me,' said the dwarf with regal simplicity.

'Can you describe him?'

'I have exceptional powers of observation coupled with the most remarkable memory in Italy since Pico della Mirandola,' he announced, glancing into the mirror with a little smile as though he were saying to his reflection, 'He doesn't know half how clever we are, does he?' Then he continued aloud, 'One metre seventy seven, I should say, and approximately seventy two kilos. What I believe is generally described as fairly good looking.' Another glance into the mirror which seemed to say, 'But hardly in *our* category.' 'Clean shaven, somewhat full lips, a chin resolute without being exactly jutting. A thick head of black hair. . . .'

Scansani had worked on various identikits in the past and had always found them frustrating and, as often as not, useless. But this was different. Amos Butturini's observation was so precise and detailed that Scansani was able to see a photographically accurate identikit coming together before his eyes.

Curiously enough he didn't identify it with the man whose appearance had caused him so much irritation the day before outside the *caffe*, but perhaps this was because his mind was entirely taken up with a single dominating thought.

What Amos Butturini was now putting together was the identikit of a killer.

A Second Helping of Spaghetti

The door of death was opened by the dragon named Emma and Peroni heard from upstairs a chatter of many voices accompanied by the sound of medieval music. It was for a single male voice, high but very sweet, accompanied with consummate skill on the lute.

The dragon stood aside to let him pass. She was no more cordial than on the previous occasion, but at least she seemed to be expecting him.

'Please follow me.'

As Peroni stepped inside, the sheer luxurious wrongness of the house struck him like a blast of hot air. Emma led him past the room where Rosalba had received him the time before and up a flight of richly-carpeted stairs.

As he went, Peroni tried to analyse his motive for coming. He wasn't in the mood for the expensive food and drink he knew he would get. In fact, he wasn't hungry at all. He was more than half drunk as a result of the various bottles of wine he had consumed with Dame Iolanthe. His hand was hurting again, he was delirious and possibly mad into the bargain. The only explanation could be that he was in search of Jacopa. Perhaps the Dame's theory had carried more weight with him than he liked to admit. And certainly, assuming there was any sense in it at all, where was time more likely to be rucked than in Jacopa's house? He looked up, half hoping to see her walking down the stairs with that look of total recognition which abolished the time gap. But Rosalba's interior decoration was far too effective. Jacopa could never have appeared in a house like that.

At the head of the stairs Emma ushered him through an arch and then retreated. Peroni found himself in a large room that occupied the entire front part of the house. At one end was a low gallery where the lutenist was accompanying his own singing and there was a small alcove just big enough for a couple to sit in comfortably. Two long tables with snowy tablecloths were

143

smothered with the most exotic copiousness of food and drink Peroni had ever seen.

This room was crowded with people in both medieval and modern dress as though they were trying to keep a visitor guessing which period he had strayed into. But there was something else about the people which puzzled Peroni, though he couldn't define it. He was trying to work this out when Rosalba joined him.

'Commissario, how delightful to see you!'

She was looking more delicately perfect than ever with a medieval dress which conveyed all her innate style, and as she gave him her hand – cool, intensely feminine and just firm enough – he felt a shudder of lust.

'A champagne cocktail?'

'*Grazie.*'

She plucked two from the tray of a passing waiter and passed one to him, delicately touching his glass with hers and smiling at him with the corners of her lips.

'I hope your investigation is progressing, Commissario?'

Did Peroni detect a shade of irony? He couldn't be sure. 'Quite well, thank you.'

'Have you discovered why the poor young man was so interested in my house?'

'I think after all,' lied Peroni, thinking that it wasn't her house but Jacopa's, 'that he really was only interested for his thesis.'

'Disappointing.'

Suddenly, in the crowd behind her, Peroni saw something that made his mouth go dry. There, drably modern among the costumed revellers, was Spaghetti, the Camorra errand-boy who had shot at him in Venice. Now Peroni realised what he couldn't define before. He had walked into a Camorra gathering. All these people were Friends or friends of Friends. How to get out before it was too late?

'I was so hoping you would disclose some exciting new factor.'

Spaghetti saw Peroni almost at the same instant, and his reaction would have been funny if the situation weren't so desperate. His features seemed to fall apart with terror and, after a second's immobility, his long limbs flailing, he immersed himself in the crowd, like a crab burying itself in the sand.

'Let me get you something to eat. Perhaps a slice of roast swan?'

'Not just for the moment, thank you.'

Getting out, he realised, wasn't going to be easy. Winding invisible cords of silk with geisha skill, Rosalba was detaining him. His mind quested desperately in search of something to cut them with.

'Ah, Commissario,' said Rosalba, apparently recognising somebody over his shoulder, 'do let me introduce you.'

It was, he realised, already too late.

They were joined by a powerful, clever-looking man in late middle age with abundant grey hair, bushy about the temples, and the sort of eyes that saw everything and forgot nothing. He was expensively dressed in modern clothes and delicately but perceptibly perfumed. A general observer might have said he was a senator. Peroni, with specialised instinct and experience, said Camorra high-up.

'Cavalier Grassi,' said Rosalba.

A Commissario, a Commendatore, a Dame, a Prince and now a Cavaliere, thought Peroni wanly, it was beginning to sound like some sort of card game.

Grassi's powerful hand shook his as though it were gripping a gun-butt.

'Commissario Peroni,' he said in a voice as smooth with menace as an iceberg, 'needs no introduction.'

It was beginning to sound, Peroni's thought continued of its own accord, as though the Cavaliere had trumped the Commissario.

'Shall we sit down?' The invitation was smooth, but there was incontestable authority behind it.

Rosalba, murmuring a lotus-petal of an apology, moved away, and the two men sat in armchairs that seemed to have been reserved for them. Peroni's mind churned. Obviously, far from not checking his police card two days previously, Rosalba had filleted the thing, and her invitation had been issued in the full knowledge that he was Achille Peroni of the Venetian *Questura*. But why? The answer to that, he knew, was not going to be long delayed.

'I hope your enquiry's making progress.' This time there could be no doubt about the irony.

'Oh, it's all just routine investigation for the moment.'

'As a matter of fact, I hadn't realised that you'd been transferred from Venice, Commissario.'

'I haven't,' said Peroni. No point in trying to talk his way round that.

'Oh.' The shortest of monosyllables which can be more loaded with meaning than an hour-long speech. So now.

'I happened to be here with a pilgrimage,' said Peroni, 'and I had met Signora Guidi. From what little I saw of her, I didn't believe she was responsible for the murder of Lorenzo Florio-Levi, so I started to make one or two enquiries of my own.'

As he talked, Peroni found himself looking at the alcove near which they were sitting. It was occupied by a young couple in medieval dress drinking champagne cocktails and looking into each other's eyes. He envied them.

'Do you still believe that Signora Guidi wasn't responsible?'

'On the whole, yes.'

'That's interesting. You see, the business has attracted my attention, too, and I've also had one or two enquiries made as a result of which I've come to the same conclusion.'

'Really?'

'Another champagne cocktail?' Cavalier Grassi flicked and two fresh glasses materialised. 'I suppose you haven't reached any conclusions about who in fact *was* responsible?'

'It's early to say.'

'Because, you see, Commissario, I have. And I wondered if you might be interested to hear who I propose as an alternative candidate.'

'Shouldn't you be telling the *Questura* in Perugia?'

'Oh, I think you should know first.'

'Why is that?'

'Quite simply because I have good reason to believe that the real killer of Lorenzo Florio-Levi was you, Commissario.'

The swallow of champagne cocktail in Peroni's gullet seemed to be transformed into a bullet of ice and the highly-coloured movement about him into stone. Just that high, sweet male voice with its lute accompaniment sang on in the nightmare as before.

'That's ridiculous,' he said at last.

'Not so ridiculous as you might suppose. Signora Guidi made a marked impression on you, and you tried on various occasions to reach an agreement with her. But she wouldn't be convinced. That must have been very irritating for you, Commissario – a man of your universally acknowledged fascination being rejected by a little bourgeois housewife. And in fact you were so irritated that, when she left the hotel by herself on Tuesday night you followed her. You saw her going into the Florio-Levi works and realised that she was with a lover. This turned your irritation into a blind fury of rage and jealousy. You broke into the house intending – well, there's no saying exactly what your intentions were, but circumstances played into your hands. Signora Guidi had left her bag in the hall of Florio-Levi's flat and, while they were inside, you examined it and found her gun. That gave you the idea for settling accounts with both of them and at the same time stepping neatly out in the middle, so to speak. You took the gun and waited for her to leave. You then shot him and left, throwing away the gun where you knew the police would find it and be led to Signora Guidi.'

Peroni realised that he had practically speaking woven his own shroud. 'You've got no witnesses,' he said, trying to sound unimpressed.

'On the contrary, a number of witnesses can testify to your deep interest in Signora Guidi. You were seen following her out of the hotel and returning after midnight, and you were also seen entering the Florio-Levi works.'

False witnesses, too, but that was only to be expected with the Camorra; nothing skimped and no expense spared.

'And there is another small point,' Cavalier Grassi continued in a tone which made Peroni feel a heave of foreboding, 'may I ask where you were last night around midnight?'

'No business of yours.' He hoped it sounded tougher than he felt.

'Perhaps not, but it may be very much yours before long. Towards midnight last night Raffaella Bonato was mown down

147

and killed by a stolen car.'

At this blow of incalculable horror, Peroni momentarily forgot his own predicament and stared in shocked grief at his mental image of the Florio-Levi secretary.

'The police,' Cavaliere Grassi was continuing, 'believe that she knew the identity of the real killer and that he, realising this, also murdered her.' He paused. 'You would have had time to get back from Rome, you know, Commissario.'

So they knew about that, too. Not for the first time Peroni had cause to wonder at Camorra efficiency.

'You said yourself a moment ago that this information should be passed on to the *Questura* in Perugia. I imagine it would be received there with some relief as the Signora Guidi theory is beginning to wear very thin, and there's nothing to take its place. On the other hand, there is no reason why this information should ever reach the *Questura*.'

He paused for Peroni to grab, but Peroni decided not to let him have that small satisfaction.

'It occurred to me that the two of us might reach a gentleman's agreement.'

Peroni considered a comment on the word 'gentleman', but decided against.

'You have been engaged for some time on an enquiry into an organisation with which I am concerned.'

For the first time Peroni became fully aware that his quest for the truth about Lorenzo had uncovered what had eluded him for so long in Venice. What did Dame Iolanthe call it? Serendipity. Even though the discovery would do nothing now but ruin him.

'It would be helpful to me if I could have a full report on your findings.'

Peroni remembered the file he had brought down to Assisi with him.

'You would, of course, be generously recompensed, and nobody but ourselves would ever know of the transaction. And I'm sure this would be only the start of a long and mutually profitable collaboration.'

A Camorra cop. Well, why not? In a society where acts of corruption were as common as cigarette stubs, what was one more or less? So why not accept the good life gracefully at last – bearing in mind that the alternative was ruin?

Unexpectedly he felt hungry and realised that he had eaten nothing since a pizza the previous evening, and at the same time, through a gap in the crowd, he saw the gargantuan medieval roasts on one of the tables, jostled by the finest European wines. All he had to do was say yes to indulge in a colossal celebratory banquet, the guest of honour, free to take his pick afterwards of the Camorra nymphets who were massed there emitting lubricity like candles on a centenarian birthday cake.

He turned to say yes, and as he did so found himself looking once again at the couple in the alcove. Yet it was not so much they as their surroundings that surprised him. The carpeting, the expensive wall-paper, the soft warm lighting were gone; so it seemed was the horribly anomalous luxury and the guzzling Camorra horde about him, and he was alone before a bare, stone alcove lit by a single candle. Then he noticed that the couple were different, too, and with a catch at the heart he recognised the russet dress.

They were talking together earnestly about something which seemed to be of great importance. And then she put her hand on her companion's arm as though to silence him for a second and turned towards Peroni. Once again total recognition flowed between them and he knew he had come to a ruck in time.

Then without transition he was back in the present. The Camorra gibbered all around, the couple in the alcove sipped champagne cocktails and ogled each other, luxury throttled Jacopa's house like pollution, and Cavalier Grassi was waiting for his answer. Peroni looked at him.

'Get fucked,' he said.

An Aerial View of Things

Coffee, short black and powerful, is an integral part of the Italian ethos. Doctors deplore it, the treasury and bar-owners exploit it, but the Italians continue to turn to it for comfort, strength and inspiration. So now, with his life in ruins and the finger of the Camorra inescapably upon him, Peroni turned to coffee.

He sat in the corner of a bar, savouring his third successive cup and reliving with trepidation the furious consternation which his exit had caused in Via Pozzo della Mensa.

And what to do now? The future was bleak indeed. And then unexpectedly the coffee made a suggestion. If, it said, he were to find out very rapidly who did kill Lorenzo Florio-Levi (and also, Peroni remembered with a chime of pure grief, Raffaella Bonato) that would effectively spike the Camorra guns and enable him to make a sensational clear-up at the same time.

The prospect began to look a shade less bleak. A double Peroni coup. The Camorra smoked out and a neat circle run round the police in Perugia. The rabbit of triumph snatched from the top-hat of catastrophe.

But the essential condition for that was the discovery of Lorenzo and Raffaella's killer, and he was still no nearer that. On the other hand, pointed out the coffee, there are elements, disparate and improbable, but elements. Juggle them, search them, interrogate them, and there was just a chance. It might be remote, but he had homed in on more than one remote chance in his time.

Somewhat heartened by these reflections, he swallowed the remains of the coffee, paid at the cash register and then, as an afterthought, went to the lavatory, a fetid hole-in-the-ground affair which, perversely, he found consoling. The door to this was separated from the cash register by a square stone pillar and it was as he was coming out and moving past this pillar that he ran straight into an express delivery of trouble.

The policeman who he had seen the previous day was showing something to the bar-owner. Peroni was just in time to step back behind the pillar without being seen and make his way quietly out through an open back door which he had noticed while going to the lavatory.

Now the future was not only bleak, but dead-ended as well. For what the policeman had been showing was an identikit of Peroni, and if he had sat personally for a portrait by Annigoni it could hardly have been more life-like. With that in circulation his chances of pursuing an enquiry were nil.

The police were closing in fast on one side and the Camorra on the other.

'Achille, I think I'm going to leave Giorgio.'

'What?'

The noise of the helicopter engine made conversation difficult. Perhaps, she thought, that was why she had picked on this absurd VIP flight to tell him; the sheer din somehow muffled her acute sense of guilt.

'I said I think I'm going to leave Giorgio,' she shouted.

'You're crazy!'

'I'm in love with Rocco!'

'Maybe, but it's your duty to sacrifice yourself.'

'Duty! That sounds good coming from you. You never give duty a thought when there's an attractive woman about!'

'I'm not married.'

'And I've never seen you all that choosy about marriage either!'

'All right then – do whatever you want! It's your business. But leave me out of it.'

They relapsed into sulky silence. Assunta was bound to admit to herself, wretchedly, that he was right. She had only told him because she had hoped to unload some of the guilt she felt, and now she resented the fact that instead of approving her decision, he condemned it as she did herself. She stared out of the window. Cumulus clouds, looking like enormous teased-out blobs of cotton wool, were beginning to mass over Umbria. Remorse set in. She had been wrong to burden Achille. Then as she glanced at his face remorse swelled into sympathy.

'What's the matter?' she asked.

He sensed the sympathy and responded to it. 'A woman I met the other day – the secretary of the Florio-Levi glassworks – was deliberately run down and killed by a car last night.'

'Oh, Achille – how dreadful!' Could this, she wondered, be the mysterious female whose presence she had guessed at, but couldn't trace? She glanced at him and decided against; his expression was of grief all right, but not that of a man who has tragically lost a woman he loves.

'But why?' she said. 'D'you mean – was it something to do with the other killing?'

'It must be. She *knew*. And if I hadn't gone away last night, she would have told me and saved her life.' He fell into a gloomy silence.

'And that's not all,' he said after a second.

'What else?'

'I'm in trouble with the Camorra. I've found the headquarters I've been looking for. Plus boss. It's too long to go into now, but he's got me into a worse corner than I've got him, even though it's a trumped up one. He wants me to hand over the findings of my enquiry.'

'And what did you say to that?'

'I told him to get fucked.'

Assunta literally trembled. She knew the Camorra and its utter ruthlessness from the days of their *scugnizzo* childhood, and she could be in no doubt about the sort of revenge Achille would have called down on his head with a provocation like that.

'And even that's not the worst of it,' he went on.

'What could be worse than that?'

'The police are after me, too.'

'Whatever for? How do you know?'

'I found out yesterday that they were making enquiries about me. Then just before we took off this afternoon I saw an identikit portrait they've got of me. Spitting image.'

'But how?'

'Somebody must have told them about the enquiries I was making – somebody who wanted me out of the way.'

'What are you going to do?'

'That's what I'm trying to work out.'

At that moment the helicopter veered sharply round and Peroni, who was sitting on the aisle, was tilted across his sister's body towards the window. Far below them, the huddle of pink and grey stone that was Assisi bucked and dipped in its lush green setting on the mountain face. Cirrus clouds had begun to mass in the high, blue Umbrian sky, but then suddenly they opened and a broad ray of sun illuminated the city like a celestial spotlight. For a moment Peroni stared out at the spectacle; then Assunta felt a violent contraction of his body. 'What's the matter?' she said, scared.

He continued to stare with the expression of someone who has been dazzled by too bright a light.

'What is it, Achille?' she tried again when he didn't answer.

He blinked as though he were having trouble in focussing on her. Then his face became uncharacteristically expressionless. 'Nothing,' he said, 'I was just admiring the view.'

But she was certain he was lying.

Assunta's Dilemma

Instinct told Zanetti immediately that the police chief had a political ace of trumps to play. The man emanated a particularly unpleasant air of smug and oily glee.

'This identikit portrait,' he said, picking it up between forefinger and thumb.

'*Si, dottore,*' said Zanetti. That could hardly be the all-powerful card. It had been obtained by Scansani from the midget television wonder whose exceptional powers of observation and memory were beyond dispute.

'The more I looked at it, the more I had the impression that I had seen this face somewhere before. You've no idea as to who it might be?'

'No, *dottore*.' Zanetti knew he was being played with and resented it deeply.

'Wouldn't like to hazard a guess?'

'No, *dottore*.'

'Well, of course, you may never have seen the person I'm thinking of, so perhaps I'm not being very fair, but I have seen him on a couple of occasions, and the resemblance is really very striking. Believe it or not,' the police chief went on, now positively skittish, 'this portrait looks to me exactly like Commissario Achille Peroni, the so-called Rudolph Valentino of the Italian police.'

153

Zanetti had never met or seen Peroni, but he felt an instinctive antipathy for him. The 'idea' of him was right-wing, and a disgraceful personality cult had been built up around him. He mustered a wintry smile. 'Really?'

'Really!'

'Remarkable.'

'Isn't it?'

The police chief laughed jovially and Zanetti, unwilling to look like a left-wing kill-joy, forced himself to join in, wondering at the same time where the conversation was leading to.

'But that's not the best of it,' the police chief went on, 'I enquired in Venice where Peroni is stationed and I learned that he is on leave at the moment. A few more enquiries revealed that he is spending this leave on a pilgrimage to Assisi with his sister.'

Zanetti's forced hilarity withered instantly on its stalk.

'It looks very much,' said the police chief, 'as though our man wasn't posing as a policeman after all. He *was* a policeman. I suggest you get in touch with him as quickly as possible.'

Exasperation as much as petrol powered Zanetti's drive from Perugia to Assisi.

'*Questura*,' he said to the lobby clerk, making it sound like a whip-crack, 'I'd like to speak to a *dott*. Achille Peroni who is staying here.'

'His group is out at the moment,' said the man, alarm showing through smoothness. 'I only came on duty a short while ago, but I imagine the gentleman you mention is with them. But I did happen to notice the lady who is with him here a short while ago. I believe she's in her room. Perhaps you would like to speak to her?'

That would be the sister, thought Zanetti. He nodded, and the lobby clerk pressed a button on the internal exchange and murmured discreetly into the mouthpiece. 'She'll be down immediately,' he said.

A couple of minutes later a pale, strained, but indisputably attractive woman arrived down the stairs, looking with interrogative anxiety towards Zanetti. Southern, of course, with all that that entailed, and bourgeois as well, but behind the anxiety and the bourgeois exterior, there was an indefinable something which seemed to glow.

'Zanetti,' he said, giving her his hand, 'perhaps we might sit down for a moment?'

She nodded and they moved to a couple of armchairs by a low, glass table.

'I am very anxious to have a word with your brother,' he said. 'Perhaps you could tell me where I could find him?'

There was a flicker of something Zanetti could not define in her dark eyes. Maybe fear.

'I'm afraid I couldn't,' she said after a brief hesitation and then, as he flashed menace like a lighthouse, she went on, choosing her words carefully, 'I don't know where he is.'

'What?'

'He's disappeared.'

It wasn't until earlier that morning that she had realised that Peroni had vanished. After the helicopter trip, he had gone off by himself saying that he had some enquiries to make, and shortly after that she had gone out with Rocco. He had taken her to a rustic-style restaurant near Perugia, all wooden benches and tables and smoke-gets-in-your-eyes from the grilling of steaks on a huge open fire. The meal and talk after it had gone on for a long time, and when she finally got back to the hotel she was tired, slightly drunk and reluctant to talk, so she had gone straight to her room.

When Achille didn't come down to breakfast the following morning she thought little of it, and even when she found that he hadn't slept in the hotel she put no great store by it, imagining that he was with the unidentified woman.

But as time went by and there was still no sign of him, alarm began to seep in. She thought of his clash with the Camorra. Lesser acts of defiance had brought swift and bloody retaliation in their wake. She thought of his hand. The idiot had still not had it seen to. What if he were ill somewhere, delirious, unable to make contact?

Her state of mind was not improved when one of her fellow pilgrims showed her a paper front-paging the identikit portrait. 'Isn't it just like your brother?' the pilgrim had said with a silly

155

laugh.

It did bear an alarming resemblance. Only the lifeless, unreal quality that all identikit portraits have prevented it from being a blazing pointer.

'Identikits are a fraud,' she had said coldly, handing the paper back.

Then upstairs in her room a new doubt had set up shop in her mind. What if Achille really had had something to do with the murder in the stained-glass works? No doubt that he had been after Signora Guidi, and however northernised he might be superficially, he still remained a Neapolitan inside with all the violence and unpredictability that entailed. And the police must have had a reason to be looking for him.

The only positive thing about this was that if they, as opposed to the Camorra, got their hands on him, she would at least quickly learn about it. It was just as she was thinking this that the desk clerk telephoned to say that a policeman wanted to see her.

'Disappeared?' said Zanetti as though she had insulted him. 'Since when?'

'Late yesterday afternoon.'

'And you've done nothing about it all this while?'

'I only realised this morning. Even then I thought – I still think – there must be some perfectly simple explanation for it.'

'Such as?'

'He may have met somebody.' Lamely. 'Stayed with them.'

'Does he usually go off without warning?'

'He's independent.'

'I presume you meant he spent the night with a woman.' Deliberately brutal.

'Maybe.'

Zanetti looked at his watch. 'It's thirteen minutes past eleven. Surely he would have established contact with you by now?'

Assunta shrugged. 'I don't know.'

'Any other possibility?'

The thought of the Camorra pulsed like a frightened heart. If Achille were being held by them, then surely she should tell this man and set the police machine in motion? On the other hand,

156

Achille was as jealous of his enquiries as of a woman, and he wouldn't thank her for revealing the culminating triumph of a long and complicated investigation to a colleague. But if his life were in danger? For a long split second she was rent with conflict between the two possible courses. The second prevailed.

'No,' she said, 'not that I can think of.'

His realisation that she was lying zig-zagged between them, and for a moment she thought he was going to renew his assault on the point. Instead he paused and then attacked from a new direction.

'What has your brother been doing since you arrived in Assisi?'

She hesitated again. 'The same as the rest of us. Visiting places.'

He paused, obviously trying to worry her, then played the next shot smoothly. 'Would it surprise you to know that he was making unauthorised enquiries into the Florio-Levi murder?'

'Well, of course I didn't know what he was doing the whole time. . . .'

'He never mentioned it to you?'

'Not that I —'

'Signora, are you trying to tell me that your brother, a policeman, didn't even mention to you a murder that occurred less than a kilometre from here?'

'He mentioned it in general terms. . . .'

'Just in general terms?' Suddenly all Zanetti's accumulated exasperation burst forth. 'You're lying!' he said, 'You're lying about his disappearance because either you know where he is or else you've got a very shrewd idea. And you're lying about his enquiries into the Florio-Levi murder, too. Do you realise that I can arrest you for withholding information?'

'Withholding *what*?' The voice came from a figure which seemed to have materialised out of the air just behind Assunta.

Bedroom with Whisky

'Withholding *what*?'

With a surge of relief, Assunta recognised Rocco's voice.

'Who are you?' said Zanetti. Extremely put out.

'The Superintendent of Fine Arts in Assisi,' said Rocco, making it sound like royalty, 'but that's beside the point. Any citizen from a dustman to the President of the Republic has the strict duty to intervene to prevent wrongful arrest.'

'This is no affair of yours,' tried Zanetti.

'Wrongful arrest is everybody's affair, and should you persist in your campaign of harrying the Signora, she is immediately entitled to a lawyer and I shall be delighted to get the best available here at once.'

It was clear that Zanetti was, temporarily, defeated.

'You'll be hearing from me again,' he said.

'I'm sure the Signora will be delighted,' said Rocco smoothly.

Zanetti left.

'That's that,' said Rocco, slipping into Neapolitan dialect as though it were a pair of comfortable slippers. 'You need a drink. What'll it be? Scotch.' He flicked across to the bar and returned with what looked like quadruple measures.

'Well, what was all that about?' he said when they were seated with their drinks.

'He's looking for Achille.'

'Whatever for?'

She told him about the identikit, noticing as she did so that her fellow pilgrims, their morning's sightseeing presumably over, were flooding back into the lobby. 'It was obvious that he was after Signora Guidi,' she concluded, 'so how can I be sure that he wasn't somehow involved? The police must have *something* to go on. And where did they get his description for the identikit?'

'Some sort of misunderstanding. Achille's not the type to kill for a woman. Where is he anyway?'

'That's the point – I don't know. I haven't seen him since yesterday afternoon.'

'What?'

She was aware of the pilgrims' eyes upon her, and it seemed that they were curious and pitying. Illogical because they couldn't know anything, but just the same she began to feel she couldn't bear it any longer.

'I've got to get away, Rocco,' she said, 'I can't stand all these people looking at me.'

'I'll take you out in the car.'

'No – I can't leave the hotel. There might be news of Achille.'

'Go up to your room then. I'll join you there in a few minutes. What number is it?'

'Seventy five. But for heaven's sake be discreet. They're curious enough about me already.'

'I'll be more than discreet – I'll be invisible.'

Assunta got up and, with eyes following her like avid mice, crossed the hall and mounted the stairs. Then a few minutes after she had reached her room there was a gentle tap at the door and Rocco appeared.

'A bottle of whisky! Oh, Rocco!'

'I lifted a couple of glasses, too. Otherwise we'd have to make do with the tooth-mug. Look, I've been thinking about Achille. The answer's simple – the lecherous sod's with a woman.'

'That's what I would have thought, too, but it's not as simple as that.' She told him about the Camorra.

'I see what you mean,' said Rocco, the network of lines on his face uncharacteristically still in gravity, 'telling a Camorra boss to get fucked isn't exactly what you'd call prudent.'

'What are we going to do, Rocco?'

'First of all drink this.' He handed her an even larger Scotch than the one downstairs. 'Did you tell the fuzz about the Camorra angle?'

'No. I was going to, but then I thought how furious Achille would be if I did. Assuming they haven't got him. But if they have —' The shadow of the unfinished sentence hung like a noose in front of her. Looking at it, she shuddered and downed the whisky.

'Try not to think about it, Assunta – though I suppose that's about the most imbecile advice anyone could give.'

Tears started to well up painfully. 'It's all my fault!' she said.

'That's a stupid thing to say! How could it be your fault?'

'I organised the wretched pilgrimage. I insisted on his coming. I was bored, and I thought we might find a bit of adventure. Look what we've got!'

The tears were born, large and hot. She felt Rocco's arms

159

about her, and let herself be pulled to him. He was as comforting as a fire on a cold night and as such, gratefully, she let herself go with him.

'If you hadn't organised the wretched pilgrimage, we should never have met again. Does that go for nothing?'

'Oh no, Rocco, you know it doesn't!'

There was movement which she didn't investigate too closely and then, without being aware of how she got there, she found herself on the bed with Rocco, and he was half kissing her, half licking away the tears. She tried to muster some sort of resistance, but the whisky and the emotional roller-coaster she was riding paralysed the attempt at interception.

'When this is over, Assunta,' she heard him saying, 'we'll go away together. Just drop everything and walk out. What do you say?'

'Oh, Rocco, if you knew how much I've longed to do that!'

There were arguments against, she knew, but she couldn't focus them because now Rocco's hands were moving about her with hot purposefulness. She felt his mouth clamping over hers and the hardness of his body, and let herself go over the precipice.

The noise came at her from a long way away. She tried to escape from it by burying herself deeper in Rocco, but it followed her. Then she realised it was the telephone, and remembered about Achille.

'*Pronto?*'

'Signora dalla Vedova?'

'*Si.*'

'One moment please. There's a call. I'll put it through.'

There was a pause, followed by a vocal explosion. '*Pronto?* Assunta?'

She closed her eyes and bit her lip so hard that blood came. It was her husband, Giorgio. '*Pronto,*' she said. 'Yes, it's me.'

'We wanted to know how you are.'

She was tempted to scream at him, heap him with insults. Maybe it was the 'we' that stopped her. 'I'm fine.'

'And Achille?'

If she told him he would drive straight down to Assisi which was the last thing she wanted now. Besides, if Achille was in the

160

hands of the Camorra, Giorgio would get to hear of it all too soon. 'He's fine,' she said.

'Both enjoying yourselves looking at old buildings, eh?'

'That's right.'

There was a pause at the other end of the line. 'Assunta, we – er – miss you.'

'I miss you.' She couldn't help it sounding so flat.

'I can't wait to see you again.' This time it was the 'I' which made her pause; Giorgio hadn't said anything as tender as that in years, and he had to choose this particular moment.

'Thanks for ringing,' she said.

'Come home soon.'

As she put the receiver down she realised that, for better or worse, the call had changed the shape of her life.

Dame Iolanthe's Little Problem

'There is only one exception to the rule that Italians will invariably vilify that which is indigenous to their native land while lauding all that which is English,' said Dame Iolanthe Higgins with the air of a high court judge ruling on a point of pure but tricky law. 'That exception,' she went on, 'concerns cooking. I have as yet to meet the Italian who will concede the smallest virtue to English food. In my time I have listened to innumerable rhapsodious encomia of things English at the expense of things Italian, at a certain point of which there invariably passes over the face of the speaker an expression of extreme distaste, usually accompanied with the phrase, 'But the food!' It is beyond my comprehension how so many well-meaning anglophiles can manage to avoid all the delights of the English kitchen.'

'One of the most outstanding lacunae of my life', said Rocco, politely sparring with the Dame in *rodomontade*, 'is that I have never visited your native land, so I can make no pronouncement.'

'You are about to be put in a position to do so,' said the Dame, 'without the necessity of crossing the Channel. Alice is going to serve what is perhaps the greatest of all English dishes.' She paused: a circus ringmaster presenting the top act in the show could not have given a better build-up. 'Steak and kidney pudding!'

Whether or not they had rehearsed it together, and Alice was waiting outside the door for her cue, there was no telling, but the fact remained that she appeared at this precise moment with a large and steaming bowl.

'Pudding, I should emphasise,' went on the Dame, 'not pie – also delicious, but a more meridional, even Frenchified version of this greatest of northern dishes. Let me serve.'

This luncheon party was the result of an unexpected encounter for which Assunta didn't know whether to be thankful or not. On the one hand, it grabbed her mind willy-nilly off other things; on the other she was scarcely in a mood for company.

After Giorgio's call had burst their erotic bubble, they had separated awkwardly, agreeing to meet at the bar outside the hotel where Assunta hoped there would be no pilgrims to spy on her. Having told the desk clerk where she was to be found, she went out there, but before Rocco had time to order a drink, they were pounced upon by a dumpy, effusive Englishwoman, dressed as a man with an outrageous floppy bow-tie and a broad-brimmed Vie Bohème hat who Assunta realised must be the eccentric lady Achille had referred to during lunch at the Excelsior.

'Commendator Palanca, my good man!' this lady roared like the entire brass section of an orchestra. 'What a delightful surprise!' Rocco had then introduced Assunta as Peroni's sister, a piece of information the lady received with theatrical awe. 'Well, I'm blasted! His sister, eh? Astonishing chap, your brother. Never known such a good looking fellow with a real brain as well – two things are normally mutually exclusive, but with him they go together as naturally as fish and chips. And talk about fish and chips, what about coming along to my place for a spot of lunch? Bring your brother along too.'

Assunta and Rocco looked at each other, and Rocco then told the Dame briefly of Peroni's disappearance.

''Pon my soul!' she said. 'Most alarming, I quite see that. But he'll turn up, don't you worry. As we English somewhat crudely put it, Signora, if your brother fell into a sewer he'd come up with a gold watch in his mouth. So come along and have a bite to eat just the same – it'll take your mind off things.'

'I'm afraid I can't,' said Assunta, 'I must stay at the hotel in case news comes.'

'No need for that,' said Dame Iolanthe grandly, 'I'll tell them to get through to me if there's anything.'

Saying this she made for the hotel, twirling her walking-stick as she went. Assunta looked at Rocco, who shrugged with palms upwards and a crooked smile. 'That's Dame Iolanthe,' he said. 'We'd better give in gracefully. I'm told the cooking at her house is excellent.'

'Deceptively soggy outside,' said Dame Iolanthe as she served the pudding, 'and steaming and sizzling like billy-ho within. *Buon appetito!*'

There was silence for a moment as the four of them savoured Alice's masterpiece. Privately Assunta thought it was disgusting.

'A masterpiece of pure Englishness!' said Rocco, and the Dame and Alice both beamed with satisfaction, apparently not noticing the equivocal nature of the assessment.

'And speaking of masterpieces,' said Dame Iolanthe, metaphorically whisking the pudding from stage centre, 'I am at the moment engaged in showing a visitor from the United States around Assisi. An Italo-American as a matter of fact, with the extraordinary name of D'Antonguolla. First time the poor chappie's been here and he's lapping up the cultural heritage like milk.'

'Indeed?' said Rocco with the expression of an eminent surgeon who sees the conversation being steered round to operations.

'Even in a country as rich in masterpieces as Italy,' the Dame went on, 'Assisi must be outstanding. Apropos of which, Commendatore, I've been meaning to telephone you with a little problem I have, but perhaps you'll allow me to take advantage of your presence here today?'

'With pleasure.'

Assunta thought she was alone in spotting a minimal

contraction of lines about Rocco's mouth indicating his reaction to shop at table.

'A glass of wine? Strictly speaking one should drink tea with steak and kidney pud, but even Alice can't get tea right out here. The water is naturally hostile. I prefer wine anyway, and even Alice's pudding couldn't be so chauvinistic as to look down on the company of a Sangiovese such as this.'

'Perfect inter-European cooperation,' said Rocco, '*Salute!*'

'Cheers!' said the Dame, putting down her glass in one, 'I really am going completely dotty in my old age – I can't remember what I was talking about.'

'Signor D'Antonguolla,' supplied Rocco helpfully.

'Ah, yes! Very knowledgeable guy, Signor D'Antonguolla. Got more European culture crammed into his head than one of Alice's stuffed marrows has got minced meat. And, like so many of these chaps, he knows more about us than we do ourselves. He will insist – and this is where I should appreciate your help, Commendatore – that there's a famous statue of Osiris here in Assisi. I keep telling him that I've never heard of any such thing, but he says that he's read about it somewhere and it must be here.'

'Osiris?' said Rocco. 'That's the Egyptian god of the dead, isn't it?'

'That's the fellow,' said the Dame, looking as pleased as if he had recognised a character in one of her novels. 'Have some more pudding.'

'No thanks – delicious though it was. No, I know of no Osiris here. He's really a bit out of character for Assisi. I mean, we've got an exceptionally rich Christian culture and a larger representation of pagan culture than most people realise. But Roman pagan. Osiris is Egyptian. I don't really see how he would have got to Italy at all.'

'The Genoese,' said the Dame vaguely, 'the Scotch of Italy with all those terribly funny jokes about meanness which I always forget.'

'I'm sorry – you've jumped beyond me.'

'No – I just meant that as one example of how a statue of Osiris could have got into Italy. The Genoese and the Venetians, too, come to that, used to go all over the world trading and so on, didn't they? And while they were at it, they used to pinch everything they could lay their hands on to take home with them – like a lot of kleptomaniacal menopausers let loose in a supermarket.' The Dame hooted with ribald laughter at this pleasantry and then stopped short with a shocked expression. 'Not very good taste, I'm afraid,' she said. 'Still, you get the point?'

'Yes, I do. And of course it's true, in theory at any rate, that there could be such a statue in Italy. But if it were, wouldn't one be likely to have heard of it?'

'History can have strange quirks. And anyway, it would seem that Signor D'Antonguolla *has* heard of it.'

'Unless he's getting his gods mixed up.'

'Neatly put. I'll suggest it to him. Well, I think we're ready for the fool, Alice.'

'Yes dear,' said Alice, getting up and collecting plates.

Assunta, already baffled by the Dame's fish-tail switches of conversation, was thrown completely off-balance by the last directive. So, to judge by his expression, was Rocco.

'A crushed fruit or the like,' explained Dame Iolanthe, apparently catching onto their bewilderment, 'scalded or stewed, according to the excellent Chambers Dictionary, mixed with cream and sugar, as, in our particular case, gooseberry. Another of Alice's specialities.'

'How do you account for that etymologically?' asked Rocco.

'Well, I don't know that I do,' said the Dame. 'It may have something in common with trifle – another of our puddings, which you Italians enigmatically define as English Soup. To fool, to trifle – the latter of course derived from the old French *trufle* which means deception. And where on earth am I to take the wretched man next?'

'I beg your pardon?'

'I'm sorry, it's my grasshopper mind. I was just wondering where I could take Signor D'Antonguolla next. Ah, here's the fool – shall we trifle with it?' Dame Iolanthe went into ecstasies of mirth over this somewhat childish sally, and it took numerous swigs of Sangiovese and anguished back-slapping by Alice to calm the ensuing fit of coughing.

'Where would you suggest?' she went on when she had recovered. 'Of course, we've already done the city itself pretty thoroughly.'

'It would take a very self-opinionated Superintendent of Fine Arts to offer sightseeing tips to anyone as well-versed in things Italian as yourself, Dame Iolanthe.'

'Quite undeserved gallantry, I'm afraid. Far from being an assiduous and systematic student of Italy, I am a mere snapper-up of unconsidered trifles — oops! there we are, King Charles's head again. Any tips you care to offer would be more than welcome.'

Rocco considered the point. 'Well, of course there's always the Robber's Den on Mount Subasio, but you know about that as well as I do. The place is practically your discovery.'

'You're absolutely right! And believe me or not, that hadn't occurred to me. Signor D'Antonguolla will be most interested in the Robber's Den. But when can we find it open? On my previous visits it's always been locked up. As my particular interest has always lain in the porch this was of no great matter, but if we're going to visit it properly —'

'You're quite right — it normally is kept locked. But I think I'm right in saying it'll be open this evening. There's some sort of an annual mass being held there. If you take Signor D'Antonguolla along afterwards you'll be able to visit the place in peace.'

'That sounds absolutely topping. We could pop up there after supper. Or would that be too late?'

'Oh, no, I don't think so. I believe the mass is at nine, so if you go up there about ten you should have it all to yourselves. I'll telephone if you like to make sure that it's kept open for you.'

'That would be jolly decent!' The Dame clapped her hands as though summoning a genie. 'This calls for Irish coffee, Alice!'

Rocco talked knowledgeably about the architecture of the chapel, obviously showing off. 'And you'll find the statue which is allegedly of the robber, Barnaba, particularly interesting. It must be late fourteenth century. It's crudely done and of no particular artistic merit, but it's got great character of its own.'

'What is this Robber's Den?' asked Assunta.

'Oh, it's a remote little chapel,' said Rocco, 'almost inaccessible at the top of Mount Subasio. I had some fresco work there restored at Dame Iolanthe's suggestion.'

'Ah, here's the coffee,' said the Dame. 'Now if you'll be so good as to pass me the Tullamore Dew, Alice, we'll Irish it. On these occasions I always think that the Italian way of describing this as corrected coffee is one of the aptest definitions in the language.'

Osiris Revealed

The man making his way up the steep, uneven rise was bent almost double into the wind which seemed to be doing everything possible to tug and pitch him off the face of Mount Subasio. He was also soaked through by the tearing, gusty rain, but he continued to climb obstinately upwards. Only once did he stop for breath and, clinging to a shrub, turn and look back the way he had come. Through the driving torrents he could make out Assisi, way below, with the lights of Perugia in the distance and the Greater Rock standing out like a threat in the night. Then he started to climb again the brief stretch that remained between him and the chapel.

The building looked deserted and defiantly locked against all comers, but when he got into the porch out of the rain and tried the handle, the door opened with an asthmatic, grating sound as though the chapel had drawn a single, painful breath. As the man stepped inside, his torch slicing through the pitch darkness picked out half a dozen ancient and rudimentary pews, a slab-like stone altar, quite bare, some fragments of frescoing on the walls: a one-legged patriarch, a dog which looked as though it were trying to remember which biblical scene it had once belonged to.

Then the beam halted on a figure standing in a glass case in the north wall of the chapel. The robber, Barnaba, in person. It was crude enough, but there was a certain peasant vigour and stolidity about it.

The man tugged over a pew and climbed up on it. The glass case turned out to be locked, but this obstacle was not insuperable, and a couple of minutes later the door swung open.

Carefully balancing his torch on the altar, the man clasped the

167

statue round the waist, and for a moment the two figures swayed together as though engaged in an all-in wrestling match. Then an equilibrium was established and Barnaba was lowered to the ground.

The man examined him carefully, then climbed back onto the pew again and probed about in the case. A curtain hung behind where Barnaba had stood and, when this was pulled aside, the torch revealed another and very different figure.

On a first glance, it seemed to be made entirely of gold, but in fact gold was no more than the background. From head to foot it was teeming with precious stones which glowed in the torchlight like super-novae exploding in a sky of pure gold.

Its richness, however, was nothing in comparison to its majesty which both stunned and hypnotised. Before this figure you knew, without any introduction, that you were in the presence of Osiris, king of the underworld. The man was so awe-struck as to be unaware of somebody else stepping into the chapel.

'*Ciao*, Signor D'Antonguolla. I was expecting you.'

Peroni turned to face Rocco, who tapped out a couple of Nazionali cigarettes for them.

'The D'Antonguolla dodge was really good,' Rocco went on. 'It gave me a bad turn when the Dame dropped Rudolph Valentino's real name into the conversation like that, and I realised that you were there all the time behind the stage, pulling the strings. Mark you, there was something slightly forced about the invitation, and I was half expecting some sort of surprise. Still,' he went on with a generous wave, 'I was pleased to know that the Camorra hadn't got their paws on you. My only regret was that I'd got used to having that thing there all to myself, and the thought of cutting you in needed some adjustment. You must admit, I did it with good grace, though.'

'You didn't have much choice.'

The lines about Rocco's mouth crowded into one of his crooked grins. 'Just like the old days all over again, isn't it? But how did you know that it was Osiris?'

'I see you haven't been to your office today.'

Rocco looked briefly taken aback. 'What's that got to do with it?'

168

'I paid a visit there last night. A very professional piece of work, I hope, but your eye wouldn't have missed traces. It took me twenty minutes to run down the missing page from Ilario's *Chronicles*. As I supposed, Lorenzo had given it to you.'

Rocco nodded. 'It was that which persuaded me to collaborate with him.'

'The reference was fairly cryptic – Jacopa de Settesoli hiding a golden god with rod and crook. But, being stationed in Venice, I knew about the group of Venetian mercenaries in the early thirteenth century who stole the legendary statue of Osiris in Egypt which subsequently vanished without trace. The dates and everything else fitted so neatly that I decided it had to be this.'

'You always were a lucky bastard, Achille. Oh well, if I've got to share with anybody, I'd just as soon it was you.'

'What makes you so sure I'm willing to make a deal?'

'Because I know you. You couldn't refuse a chance like this. It must be the most priceless treasure in the world.'

The two men looked in awe at the Egyptian king of the underworld, glowing regally in the darkness of the little chapel.

'If we break it up and sell it,' Rocco continued, 'we could be multi-millionaires!'

'You could break up *that*?'

'For that sort of money, I could break up anything.'

Peroni was silent for a second. 'How do we handle it?'

'Simple. First sell some of the less conspicuous stuff. Nothing to arouse comment, but enough to raise four or five billion lire. With our contacts that should be no trouble. Then go to South America – somewhere like that and take our time selling off the rest.'

Peroni had never actually taken a bribe. He had considered the idea, sometimes very seriously, and in the end had always rejected it. But he had always had the uneasy feeling that somewhere at the end of the line the Big Bribe was waiting for him with a Mona Lisa smile on its lips. And here it was.

'And leave everything behind?' His voice came from a great distance.

'Leave *what* behind?' Peroni had never heard Rocco speak so bitterly. 'For me,' he went on, 'everything is a shrewish, half mad wife and a stuffed dummy job. For Assunta, a fat bore of a husband, a couple of grasping teenage children and a round-the-clock unpaid job as household drudge. And you?'

Rocco didn't need to recite the list. A job, under-paid and under-valued, uncomfortable and often dangerous in a police force hag-ridden by politicians. A rented apartment in a damp and crumbling *palazzo* near the fruit and vegetable market in Venice. A perch with his sister's family in Verona on such occasions as a crushing work-load allowed him to go there. So what had he got to lose?

'No,' he heard himself saying, still in the distance, 'I'm not leaving.'

'Principles, Achille?' The network of lining on his face arranged itself in a quizzical pattern.

But something else was going on in Achille's mind, and it fished up a memory from the distant past. One April the first, long ago in Naples, Rocco had succeeded in pinning a paper April fish on Peroni's back, and he had gone about for nearly an hour without being able to trace the source of the amusement he was arousing.

Rocco must have caught hold of the same memory, for he said, 'D'you want me to tell you what the fish is this time?'

Peroni shrugged, feigning indifference.

'Or shall I keep it to myself?' Peroni waited. 'No, it's too good to keep a secret. You see that great golden god of death, tempested with precious stones?' In spite of himself Peroni looked at Osiris again. 'You know what? It's a fake.'

However reluctant he was to give Rocco satisfaction, Peroni was unable to hide astoundment. 'A fake?'

'A king-sized, or perhaps I should say a god-sized fake. Probably the greatest fake in history.'

'So it's worth nothing?'

'Oh, I wouldn't say that. There's a certain amount of real gold, and as a work of art it's probably worth a good deal. But the difference between that and the sort of money we were talking about is measurable in light years.'

'But what happened to the original?'

'Who knows? But if you want my guess, the Venetian ambassador, Morosino, nicked it and had some master craftsman

170

from Murano make this which he put in its place. It fooled me, so why shouldn't it have fooled the recipient then? The whole thing must have been a brilliant gamble. It wasn't meant to withstand detailed, expert examination.'

Peroni thought for a moment. 'If it's a fake,' he said, 'why bother to go through all that performance with me?'

Rocco lifted his hands in the air, palms upmost, in the eternal Neapolitan what-would-you? gesture. 'Amusement. And I was curious to see how much strain your integrity would take before snapping.'

'And when it didn't snap?'

'I wasn't too worried. I knew I had a better offer in reserve.'

Peroni felt a snap of apprehension. 'What offer?'

'The redemption of your soul. Of all our three souls. I didn't realise it before, but curiously enough it really wasn't so much the money that mattered. It was the chance to become what I was before respectability caught up with me. And for you and me and Assunta that chance is still waiting to be picked up. We can be the three musketeers again, ranging the world untrammelled.'

Just for a second that really was a worse temptation, but at the same time Peroni felt there was something wrong with it, though he couldn't immediately define what. Then he got it. The whole thing was childish bombast. 'Three musketeers again, ranging the world untrammelled.' Windy rhetoric. And with that realisation, a lot of things that should have been there leapt into the forefront of his mind.

'Do you really think,' he said, 'that our relationship could go back to what it was?'

'Why not?' For the first time there was a trace of unease in his tone.

'You could convince me into forgiving you a lot, Rocco,' said Peroni, 'you always could. But even you can't make me forgive you for killing a lover, unprepared and unarmed.'

'A lover?' The smile was still just there.

'Raffaella Bonato. Last Friday she started to tell me about a key to the Florio-Levi works that she had lost, but at the last minute she clammed up. Out of loyalty to you, Rocco. She must have decided to give you the chance to defend yourself first and

171

ask you whether you had taken the key from her bag. And you did defend yourself. You ran her over on Friday night.'

'You're over-reaching yourself, Achille. Raffaella Bonato was no more than an acquaintance. I couldn't have taken a key from her bag.'

'Raffaella was your mistress. When I first met her, I noticed a plate from the Wolf Hotel in Gubbio hanging in her office, and when I asked her about it she said she often stayed there. It struck me as odd at the time that somebody living in Assisi should spend the money to stay "often" at a hotel in a town so relatively near. It sounded like a love affair which she, or the man, or both, wanted to keep secret. So while I was sorting things out in my mind at Dame Iolanthe's I made some enquiries and discovered that you and she used to stay there together.'

Rocco seemed to scrutinise the situation with an expert eye as though it were a crumbling arch to be shorn up. The lines in his face jostled enigmatically. 'How did you know?'

'I think I knew it was you, Rocco, even before there was anything to know. The first night when we were in Assisi and I followed Signora Guidi to the Florio-Levi works I knew that somebody else was following me, but I couldn't flush anybody. You're the only person in the world who could do that to me. Then later when the police started looking for me, I realised that somebody must have tipped them off and nobody except you would have done that. But I still didn't know what it was all about and I had no proof.'

Rocco thought again. 'OK,' he said, 'what are you going to do?'

'I'm going to arrest you. Then it's up to the examining magistrate and tribunal.'

'So you really are a cop?'

'I'm what life's made me. And life includes you.'

'What if I resist arrest?'

Almost as if by magic a gun appeared in Peroni's hand.

'Let's go.'

Rocco took a couple of steps towards the door, then stopped and turned to face Peroni. 'The last duel,' he said, 'I suppose it started that morning last week when we met in the basilica. I know that you know that I know that you know. And some clever twists. But I suppose this is the end.' He started to turn again, then stopped, apparently hesitant. 'And then again,' he said, 'I wonder. You know those telly bang-bang films when the cop's there with a gun in his fist, and the baddie's standing there all of a sudden transformed into a puppet. "Stick up your hands," says the cop, and the baddie does. "Start walking," says the cop, and the baddie starts walking. And all because of that thing you've got in your hand. Well, d'you know, I've often wondered why that thing can transform baddies so drastically into puppets. OK, I know – you don't do like I say, Mac, and you get dead. But do you? Maybe cops don't always make those things go bang quite so easily. Maybe they're reluctant to use them. Maybe they're even scared. You know what, Achille? I reckon you're not exactly falling over yourself to pull that trigger.'

The trouble is he's right, thought Peroni. Few people realise the truth of it, but when they do the gun loses nine-tenths of its power.

'Have you ever killed anyone, Achille?'

Yes, once – a terrorist in a smoke-filled church in Verona. I couldn't sleep for a month afterwards. Don't let him see how right he is.

'Your hand's pretty steady, but your mind isn't.'

Rocco had taken a step forward.

'You're not going to use that thing, are you, Achille?'

Another step. Shoot at his legs, you fool. Warn first, then shoot. He opened his mouth to pronounce the warning, but for some reason the words wouldn't come. Then, too late, he remembered Rocco's power as a hypnotist. He had seen it at work on other people in the old days, admired it, envied it, Now it was being used on him.

'You're not going to use it. You're not going to use it.'

Skip the warning – just shoot!

'You're not going to use it. . . .'

Peroni tried to contract his right index finger, but it wouldn't move.

'You're not going to use it. . . .'

Rocco is a killer – shoot!

173

Then suddenly Rocco leapt. Through Peroni's mind there flashed the image of a tiger leaping, and this liberated it from the hypnotic torpor. But too late. Rocco's body crashed into his.

Under normal circumstances they would have been fairly equally matched. Rocco was a little heavier, but Peroni was in better training. The circumstances, however, were not normal. Peroni's left hand had been seen to while he had been staying at Dame Iolanthe's, but it was still far from fighting efficiency. The struggle was brief. In spite of his years as a Superintendent of Fine Arts, Rocco had forgotten even less of the tricks they had learned in the gutters of Naples than Peroni had, and these together with Peroni's handicap gave him quick victory. Peroni felt himself being violently twisted back and downwards, and he hit the chapel floor hard. When he was in a position to register again, Rocco was standing over him with the gun.

'You always did have a Hamletic streak about you, Achille. So there *was* another twist after all. It'll take them some while to find your body dumped in some crevasse hereabouts. With a bit of luck they never will. And if they do – well, everyone knows that's the way bodies end up after a Camorra execution. No loose ends. *Ciao*, Achille.'

Peroni had no doubt whatsoever that Rocco would shoot. There had never been a trace of ruth in him, and he had already killed twice in the past week. St Januarius, Peroni invoked, St Januarius.

The blast of gunshot roared appallingly in the little chapel. Peroni wondered that you were in time to hear it before you exploded. Then wondered that you could wonder. Then opened his eyes.

The sight was surreal. Rocco was still standing above him, but swaying slightly, apparently oblivious of Peroni's existence and with his ugly face transformed by sheer amazement. Then there was a hard clatter as the gun fell on the stone floor, and at the same time Rocco started to pitch forward. As he toppled, Peroni looked wildly about for some explanation, and when he found one almost wished that things had not so fallen.

Assunta appeared out of the blackness near the door with a gun in her hand, her face a stone mask of horror. She walked

174

towards Rocco as if she were asleep and then, when she reached him, crumpled onto her knees, and at the same time there came from her a sort of animal moaning.

Then Peroni saw that Rocco's lips were moving, though no sound emerged. He was trying to say something to Assunta. Peroni moved nearer just in time to catch a phrase, breathed more than spoken.

'Who said – women can't aim?'

Rocco's mouth stretched into its last grin. His eyes moved, searching, and fixed on Peroni.

'You lucky ba —'

Death interrupted the phrase and the lines on Rocco's face settled into repose.

Valentino Rides Again

Assunta was under heavy sedation, but that didn't prevent her from being intensely aware of the presence of two men. One was sitting on a chair outside the door. He was a *Carabiniere*, and his presence meant that she was under arrest. The other was her husband, Giorgio. She knew he was sitting there beside her, watching over her, pathetically anxious for a sign of recognition. But shame and self-disgust made her hide from him in feigned unconsciousness.

And although she tried to stop it, the succession of events leading up to Rocco's death played itself through in her mind, over and over again, as though on some demented cinema projector. The sequence always started at exactly the same point. There she was at the table in Dame Iolanthe's doll's house dining-room with a fork of the disgusting steak and kidney pudding half way to her mouth, following the conversation with bewildered curiosity, when suddenly a sentence pronounced by the Dame sliced into her mind like a cleaver.

'An Italo-American as a matter of fact with the extraordinary name of D'Antonguolla.'

The name with which Rudolph Valentino had been born.

This could only mean one thing. Achille, under the pseudonym of D'Antonguolla, was speaking through the Dame.

Her first reaction of delighted relief was immediately capped by puzzlement. What was going on? If Achille were getting some sort of message through, which is what it sounded like, for which of them was it intended? Had Rocco caught the allusion? He could hardly have failed to, and yet he gave no sign. Did he realise that she had caught it? Perhaps not. The cult had been an extravagance of the two boys (she had always considered it silly and had never understood what women used to see in Valentino) so there was no reason why he should imagine that she had understood. She decided to keep quiet and see if she could make out what was going on.

Then there had been the curious conversation about the Osiris. There was something not quite right about that, as though the fabric of the conversation were being stretched too tight. And finally the reference to the Robber's Den with a mass at nine. Would a mass be held at such an out of the way place so late in the evening? 'If you go up there about ten you should have it all to yourselves.' That sounded suspiciously like an appointment.

Assunta decided to go on saying nothing and to be at the appointment herself to find out what it was all about.

Her suspicion had become rampant when Rocco, who had hitherto scarcely left her side, had said that he had to be away on unavoidable business that evening.

She enquired where the Robber's Den was, took a taxi to within striking distance of it, told the driver to wait for her and then in the darkness and pouring rain scrambled to within sight of the little chapel. The ragged forest about it, she was pleased to notice, would allow her to hide or move about unobserved as much as she wished.

Around nine Rocco arrived, and she watched him going into the porch and unlocking the door within. He then re-emerged and disappeared among the trees on the other side of the building. By now her curiosity was ravenous. The whole thing made her think of the secret, complex sparring that used to go on between her brother and Rocco in Naples. But what could be behind it? Almost unaware of the fact that she was soaked to the skin, Assunta waited on in the darkness.

There was a longish wait, and then another figure came into sight which Assunta recognised as her brother. He struggled up the steep slope against wind and rain, and disappeared into the chapel.

After a couple of minutes there was a stirring in the trees opposite and Rocco emerged and followed Achille inside. She waited for a while and then moved quietly into the porch. The door had not been pulled to so it was easy to hear the two of them talking together.

'. . . . if I've got to share with anybody, I'd rather it was you than anybody else.'

Then talk of 'the most priceless piece of treasure in the world' – Osiris? – and escape to South America which gave her a great lift of exhilaration.

'. . . . a fat bore of a husband, a couple of grasping teenage children and a round-the-clock unpaid job as household drudge. . . .'

For a woman on the brink of leaving her family, it was surprising how badly that hurt.

'You know what? It's a fake.'

Just like Rocco to prick a balloon that he himself had blown up.

The talk ebbed and flowed, and she was beginning to feel a strange detachment when Achille said something that injected her with sudden horror.

'. . . . even you can't make me forgive you for killing a lover, unprepared and unarmed.' As she listened a sense of horror and betrayal exploded within her. Impotent, terrified, mountingly appalled, she continued to listen. The arrest. The gun. Rocco's voice, lilting, soothing. Hypnotism. She remembered his mastery of it and knew he would get the gun.

She stepped through the door into the shadows within just in time to see Rocco's leap and seizure of the gun. She was in no doubt at all that he was going to kill Achille.

Whether the desire to save her brother or her own sense of betrayal had the upper hand she would never know, but almost without knowing what she was doing she felt in her bag for the gun that Giorgio made her carry because of the alarming increase of muggings and assaults in drug-ridden Verona.

Out of the darkness, she pointed it at Rocco and pulled the trigger. The explosion seemed to come to her from another world as the scene played itself remorselessly through in her mind and, opening her eyes to avoid the vision of Rocco's death, she saw Giorgio's face looking down at her, filled with more pain than she had ever thought him capable of.

'I'm sorry,' she heard herself say.

'There's nothing to be sorry about.'

Of course, he didn't know that part of it. But it made no difference. How could you go on living with somebody after such a betrayal, whether they knew or not?

'Try not to worry,' Giorgio went on. 'About anything.'

Strange that it should have taken something like this to make her realise how much she did love him. And her grasping teenage children. Even her unpaid job as a household drudge. Too late.

There was a knock at the door, and the *Carabiniere* guard opened it to admit Achille.

'*Ciao*,' he said. 'How d'you feel?'

'Better.'

Her husband's face lit up with delight. 'Good,' he said, 'because we all need her – don't we, Achille?'

'Yes.' Uncharacteristically monosyllabic. But his look said more, telling her that Giorgio would never know about her and Rocco unless she cared to tell him. She looked back her gratitude.

'When will she be free to travel?'

'There should be a formal order through from the magistrature authorising provisional liberty in the next couple of days,' said Peroni.

'That'll be just splendid,' said Giorgio and went on, turning to Assunta, 'you'll feel much better when you get home, won't you?'

She looked from him to her brother and back again. Maybe it wasn't too late after all.

Beyond Osiris

'Sugar or lemon, Commissario?'

'Lemon, please.'

In spite of his love for things British, Peroni detested tea and would certainly have refused it now if it hadn't been Signora Guidi who was pouring it out.

'I wish I knew how to express my gratitude,' she said, passing him the cup and looking into his eyes with her china-blue ones and an expression that suggested the princess thanking St George after having been rescued from the dragon.

'I was only doing my job,' said Peroni, dropping automatically into a rather unconvincing Perry Mason act. The look she continued to give him was an ointment of pure pleasure.

'I, too, wish that I could better express our gratitude.' Unfortunately, there was a fly in the ointment in the person of the Signora's husband, *Avv.* Guidi, a punctilious, irritable little man, about ten years older than his wife, who always seemed to be addressing a tribunal. 'However,' he went on, 'I am bound to confess that I am completely at a loss to understand what has been going on. There are the wildest stories circulating about a statue and a young German murdered in the thirteenth century. I should be relieved if you could elucidate matters for us.'

'Oh, please explain it all, Commissario,' his wife chimed in prettily, 'I do feel so confused.'

Peroni started to swell, then switched to appealing modesty as being more effective. 'When you were arrested, Signora,' he said, 'I immediately had the impression that something was wrong. I just didn't believe that you could —' He checked himself hastily. 'I didn't believe that you could have done it.' She lowered her eyelids in modest confirmation. 'So I started to look for something else that might have led to his death, and I found that he'd been researching into medieval Assisi with surprising enthusiasm and thoroughness. In particular into the life of a lady called Jacopa de Settesoli – a Roman noblewoman who was a close friend of St Francis. I decided to follow his research and see where it led. And it led, along a variety of corridors, to a particular date – 25th May 1230. On that day the lower of the two churches which make up the basilica of St Francis was opened, and at the same time Francis's body was transferred to the crypt there from the church of San Giorgio where it had been lying until then.

'People came for the ceremony from all over Europe, and many of the Italian city states sent embassies. Including Venice. This Venetian embassy was headed by a certain Bartolomeo Morosino, and it included two men who both must have played significant parts in the story as I think it can be constructed. One was a young nobleman called Michele Aquila. The other was a German, Corrado di Turingia, who appears to have been the lover of the ambassador, Morosino.'

Signora Guidi's eyes dropped at this and her husband cleared his throat.

'Those are the human ingredients that Lorenzo researched. And when they were all brought together, they resulted in murder.' Peroni paused for effect; he was in his element.

'At this point another figure comes into the story – a town crier of Assisi, named Ilario and nicknamed the Rubicund. He must have been quite a character – an amateur versifier and incurable gossip, one knows the type, who combined these two by writing a highly scurrilous verse history of Assisi in that period. Most of it needs taking with several packets of salt, but even Ilario could hardly invent a body, and he says very clearly that the German, Corrado, was murdered in the upper chamber of the Lesser Rock – where the Venetian embassy was lodged, and where you, Signora, were arrested last week.

'It seemed to me that this murder was the crux of the whole thing. That until I discovered who murdered the young German – or more exactly perhaps why he was murdered – I would never understand who murdered Lorenzo Florio-Levi seven centuries later.'

He paused to let that *colpo di teatro* take full effect.

'The news of this murder was in an eighteenth century handwritten copy of the Ilario *Chronicles*, pieced together from the

180

previous oral tradition, and the only one of its kind in existence. But Lorenzo had been there before me, and a page had been removed from it. It seemed very probable that that page contained a mention of whatever it was that linked the two murders.

'Shortly after this I was running through it all with a friend of mine here in Assisi, the English writer, Dame Iolanthe Higgins – maybe you've heard of her? No, well, it doesn't matter. Anyway, it was she who pointed out to me the very important fact that whatever the link was, it had to be a thing and not a person because only things can last for seven centuries. But the nature of that thing was a complete mystery, and when I mentioned that to her, she said something else of great significance. A mystery, she said, is something in itself dark which sheds light on everything around it.

'And it almost seemed as though it did shed a certain amount of light – in my mind anyway. I knew that something of great value must be involved because two murders – three if you include the secretary of the Florio-Levi glass works – had been committed for it. And I knew from the direction of Lorenzo's research that Jacopa de Settesoli was somehow involved. But I'd already found out all I could about her life without learning any more of this mysterious thing. Then I remembered reading some fragments of letters of hers written to her two sons in Rome, both of whom were here in Assisi in May 1230, and I wondered whether maybe their careers might reveal something of the nature of the thing.

'Following this line of thought I discovered that the younger of the two, Graziano, had been killed while mounting a sort of commando assault on the New Church in Assisi. That seemed like a big step forward. Whatever-it-was of such great value had been hidden in the New Church. Graziano had died trying to get hold of it. Lorenzo had found out about it and also been killed because of it. But when I went to see the New Church all that reasoning collapsed because the building is seventeenth century baroque. It just wasn't there in 1230.

'But later that day I happened to go for a helicopter trip of the area and, looking out of the window, I saw something which explained everything. What I saw was the basilica of St Francis, lower church and upper church and, seen from the air, there could be no doubt about it. For centuries the only conceivable "new" church in Assisi could only have been the upper one – the one frescoed by Giotto.

'And then everything fell into place. Lorenzo had obviously made the same deduction as I had about the "new" church and then realised that Commendator Palanca was already installed there with his assistants, shoring up the building with its precious frescoes against earthquake damage.

'In one sense, this must have seemed like a great stroke of luck – the possibility of expert help and equipment to get the thing out. On the other hand, it meant sharing the profit. But he didn't have much choice – he could never have got it out by himself. So he put the case to Commendator Palanca.'

Peroni paused, and when he resumed, his tone was colourless. 'I happened to know Palanca years ago in Naples, and I can imagine how enthusiastic he must have been. He was always on the look out for a fortune. So the two of them worked together on the project by night. It can have been no great problem. Much of the floor was already taken up, and if any of the friars chanced to look in, what could have been more natural than for the Superintendent of Fine Arts to be putting in a little extra work on a vital project with his young assistant?

'All this became more or less clear during the helicopter flight, but by then my own position was such that there was nothing I could do about it. For various reasons, both the police and the Camorra were after me, so I decided that my only chance was to disappear and try to sort things out in hiding.

'Thanks to the hospitality of Dame Iolanthe this was no problem, and one or two enquiries I made from her house confirmed what I had already realised – that Palanca had killed Lorenzo to gain exclusive possession of some object, and later killed Raffaella Bonato because she was aware of this. What I didn't know was the nature of the object. So I paid a visit of somewhat dubious orthodoxy to Commendator Palanca's office. There I found, as I suspected I might, the missing page from Ilario's *Chronicles* which told me that the object hidden in the "new" church was a literally priceless statue of Osiris.'

For some while now there had been a sound as of heavy rain, but as the sun was shining brightly outside, Peroni looked about him for some other explanation, and found it in the fingers of *Avv.* Guidi's right hand, which were drumming uninterruptedly on the arm of his leather armchair, and at this point, apparently unable to bear it any longer, he burst out in lawyer-like exasperation, 'But what is all this about, Commissario? What was this statue of Osiris doing in Assisi at all? What's the point of the whole business?'

'That worried me for a long time,' said Peroni. 'It was my friend Dame Iolanthe's definition of a mystery that made me understand the truth at last. I'd been thinking all along that the mystery was Osiris, but Osiris shed no light around him. There had to be something else, something beyond Osiris, so to speak. And strangely enough that something beyond was at the back of my mind the whole time. Yours, too, Signora, come to that.'

'Mine?' Signora Guidi looked as scared as if he had suddenly passed her a hand-grenade with the pin out.

'During our first visit to the basilica,' said Peroni, 'when we were in the crypt, don Sereno told us about the truly incalculable value of relics in the Middle Ages. When I remembered that, I understood. The mystery which shed light on everything around it was little more than a handful of dust. It was the mortal remains of St Francis.'

Jacopa's Valediction

When Peroni detonated this narrative bombshell, *Avv.* Guidi and his wife looked at each other the way couples who have been married for some while automatically exchange glances in the face of the unusual, and observing them Peroni became aware of something that had been niggling at him since the beginning of this expository tea-party. The lawyer was a sharp, shrewd man who plainly not only stood but planted himself on his rights, and yet he seemed to be quite unconcerned about his wife's infidelity with Lorenzo. If that hadn't been impossible Peroni would even have said that he was unaware of it.

'You mean the Venetians —?' said the *avvocato*, interrupting Peroni's bewildered speculation.

'Exactly. Of course they already had the remains of St Mark, but they'd had them for some while by then, and familiarity, even with one of the four evangelists, breeds, if not exactly contempt, at least a certain indifference. And the prestige of St Francis at the time of his death was probably higher than that of any other saint in the entire history of Christianity. With him in their hands, the Venetians would have had a sort of everlasting poker in the international as well as the national game.'

'And Osiris was the *quid pro quo*?'

'That's right.'

'But if, as I understand, the statue was a fake?'

'One of the most brilliant fakes ever made. Even Commendator Palanca didn't discover it until he'd made a thorough examination.'

'But why a fake? What happened?'

'Exactly what happened we shall never know, but we can reconstruct approximately. I strongly suspect that the villain of the piece was the Captain of the People in Assisi at the time, a man called Ugo da Palazzo. He sounds the type, but he was also the only man in the right position.

'One of Jacopa's letters shows that the Venetian embassy was in Assisi some while *before* the great ceremony in May 1230. I imagine it was there for secret negotiations with Ugo. The body of Francis was to be laid out in the church of San Giorgio on the night between the 24th and 25th of May prior to its removal to the basilica next day. The Venetians wanted Ugo's assistance in stealing it during that night. And he agreed to give it – in exchange for Osiris.

'The operation was in the hands of this man, Morosino, who was something like the head of the Venetian KGB. Whether the idea of the fake originated with the Venetian government – they would have been quite capable of it if they'd thought they could get away with it – or whether it was Morosino's own private initiative there's no telling. His sudden and mysterious eclipse from the Venetian political scene suggests the latter, but it's anybody's guess. Maybe the original will turn up one day and clarify the situation.

'Anyway, the fake was made and carried with the embassy down to Assisi. The idea was presumably that it should be handed over to Messer Ugo who, in the chaos preceding the 25th of May would hardly have been able to make a detailed technical examination – even if the idea of a fake had ever occurred to him. He would then have helped the Venetians in their theft of the body and finally, I daresay, made a quick getaway himself. But things didn't happen like that.

'We know that a childhood friend of Jacopa's, Michele Aquila, was part of the embassy. He was in love with her and so we can assume that he told her of the plot, and the two of them, probably with her sons as well, decided that the simplest way to defend the body of Francis, and the one least likely to cause bloodshed, was to remove the Osiris which would automatically block the transaction. But how? It was kept under constant guard in the Lesser Rock which must have seemed completely inaccessible.

'Here again we have to speculate. Some time between the arrival of the embassy and the moment agreed for the handing over of the statue, which Morosino must have deferred to the last minute to give Ugo as little time as possible to spot the fake, Morosino himself and the rest of the embassy were at some function in the town, leaving the German, Corrado, behind on guard. Michele will have told Jacopa this, and somebody went out to the Lesser Rock.'

'But who?' As sharp as if he were cross-examining.

'My guess is Jacopa's sons. In one of her letters she mentions the exceptional courage of the elder, Giovanni.'

'You're suggesting they went up there, killed the German and removed the statue?'

'More or less.'

'But how did they get into the tower? It would certainly have been locked.'

'I think one of them, Giovanni, got in through the window at the top.'

'But that's impossible!' spluttered the lawyer.

'That's what I thought myself, but then I remembered having seen a film clip of a climber negotiating a sheer, vertical rock face of Mount Cervino and I realised that, compared with that, the Lesser Rock is a pushover. It's full of grooves and crevasses. You or I might not care to climb it –' Peroni caught on the wing Signora Guidi's look which said she was quite sure *he* would. '– but a young man like Giovanni using some sort of sling and climbing pick could have done it. And the fact remains that somebody did.'

'And from there to the foundations of the "new" upper church?'

Peroni smiled. 'I don't think that anybody except Morosino himself would have known the statue was a fake. They must have all thought it was priceless.'

'Exactly!' The word sounded like the springing of a mouse-trap. 'Then nobody would have been so crazy as to hide it where it would never be found again.'

Peroni's smile lingered. 'One person would.'

'Who?'

'Jacopa de Settesoli. She had her ideas about money from her old friend, St Francis, who considered it – if you'll forgive the word, Signora – *merda*. She must have thought for quite a while about where she could hide it safely, out of the reach of human greed. And then she thought of the basilica. Lower church already done, upper one starting to go up as fast as Brother Elias could push it. Another raid – this time presumably by night, and Osiris was embedded deep in the foundations. The idea must have appealed to Jacopa's sense of humour. She'd never really liked the building.'

'You talk as though you knew her.'

'There are times when I almost feel as though I do. Anyway, that's the story as I reconstruct it.'

'And a most absorbing one, I am bound to concede,' said the lawyer. He looked at his watch. 'I must thank you for giving us your valuable time, Commissario.' He got up and shook Peroni's hand. 'My wife and I really must be starting back for Verona.'

'Just one moment, dear,' his wife interrupted him, 'There's something I should like to ask the Commissario.' She turned to

Peroni. 'The police told me that Commendator Palanca came into the Florio-Levi building after me on that terrible night, that he was hiding there when I left —' she shuddered prettily at the thought '— and that he then shot poor Signor Florio-Levi. But how did he ever know that I was going there that evening? He couldn't have just been there by chance.'

She's sailing into dangerous waters, Peroni thought to himself. Aloud he said, phrasing it as cautiously as he could, 'I managed to clear that up while I was in hiding at Dame Iolanthe's. You remember that you attended a medieval history congress in Verona last year?'

'Yes, of course. That was when we met Signor Florio-Levi.'

She seemed to be deliberately drawing it to her husband's attention.

'Well, Commendator Palanca was also present at that congress. He saw you there.' How to put it without igniting the rocket of awareness in the cuckolded lawyer's head? 'He saw you with Florio-Levi, so when he saw you again in the basilica last week, he assumed that you would be meeting again. And he was waiting for you.' He came to an end, more than half expecting a bellow of outraged marital wrath.

'An agreeable young man,' said *Avv.* Guidi instead. 'We found at the congress that we had a shared interest in Barbarossa. In fact, if it hadn't been for that, this whole sad business wouldn't have occurred.'

'I don't quite follow,' said Peroni, utterly nonplussed.

'My wife,' the lawyer explained, 'called on Florio-Levi to ask him for some material about Barbarossa for me.'

'To ask —?'

'Quite so. Didn't you know? That was her motive for going to the Florio-Levi works last week.'

'Yes, of course,' said Peroni, 'I was forgetting.'

Signora Guidi gave Peroni her hand and, with it, a little smile of pure complicity. 'I am so grateful to you, Commissario,' she said, 'for everything.'

Not for the first time, Peroni wondered whether there were any limits to what a woman could make a man believe if she set her mind to it.

Two marriages patched up, thought Peroni, and Assunta's at any rate set fair to run the rest of its course without serious incident. He wasn't quite so sure about Signora Guidi; for a wife who had had such an exceptionally narrow squeak she was looking altogether too chipper, and Peroni was not at all sure that he didn't have an unspoken invitation for next time he was in Verona. Still, for the moment two marriages had been patched up, four human beings united once more with their respective partners. And Peroni himself once more out on a limb. Pig in the middle.

This sense of isolation made him feel more acutely than usual the conflict within himself. He now knew for sure that the Commissario could never eliminate the *scugnizzo*, and the *scugnizzo* could never suppress the Commissario. Harmony would never be achieved, so they must continue to lacerate each other for ever. The prospect was infinitely depressing.

He left the hotel where he had had tea with the Guidis and walked to the little house in Via Pozzo della Mensa and let himself in.

When, two days previously, he had finally cleared up his own position with the police and gone with a couple of assistants to the medieval house that had once been Jacopa's he found that Cavalier Grassi and Rosalba had skipped, which came as no great surprise to him. He knew from experience that even when you made a major strike against the Camorra you rarely got the top men. But in that sort of struggle it was still a victory; Grassi could never again be a giant pike lurking anonymously on the river bed. He was blown for good. And the lead he provided led to a series of arrests, including that of Spaghetti, who had in fact been carrying information concerning the entire Grassi-Camorra network when he had bumped into Peroni in Venice.

The house in Via Pozzo della Mensa had already been meticulously gone over, and Peroni's motives in returning now were mixed. Above all, he needed to be active, but he knew, too, that one more search was seldom a waste of time. If nothing else it occasionally produced a point of view.

The house was in pitch darkness and, before switching on any lights, he stood for a moment, feeling the mood of it, and it seemed to him as though the old building, after having its character wrenched out of true by Rosalba, was beginning to be itself again. He switched on the lights and went up the stairs.

He started on the room where Grassi had slept when he hadn't wished for company, then went to Rosalba's room, which was still so redolent of her geisha-like voluptuousness that he felt a painful jab of lust. He sat at her dressing table beside the little medieval window, deep set in the wall, and imagined that he could see her face in the gold-framed mirror.

Looking away he found himself examining the window-ledge. No, not the ledge itself, but something below it and almost entirely hidden by it. It was an irregularity in the wall, covered by Rosalba's expensive wall-paper, and he wouldn't have been able to see it at all if he hadn't been seated at the dressing table. He got a pair of nail-scissors and cut away some of the wall-paper only to find that the irregularity, a slight protuberance, had been plastered over. He decided to risk a little superficial demolition and, having located a hammer and chisel, started to chip away at the plastering.

In less than a minute the protuberance was revealed as a rudimentary embrasure – one of the semi-secret crannies that medieval builders delighted in. It seemed to be empty, but it was fairly deep, a miniature domestic cave, and feeling inside Peroni's hand came into contact with paper.

It was a single sheet and, taking it out, his mouth went suddenly dry with excitement. The handwriting on it belonged unmistakably to Jacopa de Settesoli.

Pushing the contents off the dressing table, he put the sheet – ancient, yellow and incredibly brittle – in their place and stared at it with a mixture of awe and perplexity. He would never be able to decipher medieval Italian in an almost archaic script.

But as he looked, one or two words seemed to stand out in relief. '*Senza di te . . . il male . . . superato. . . .*' Without you. Evil. Overcome. Without you evil would not have been overcome. This must be a letter, he realised, or the draft of a letter Jacopa had written to Michele Aquila after the scheme for snatching the body of St Francis had been blocked.

189

'Continue to overcome.' That was quite clear.

Skipping here and there, interpolating, guessing, linking, Peroni began to piece together a rough and ready translation into modern Italian.

'You doubt yourself. You are a great man without, but you know that there is an irreverent small boy within. I have always seen that little boy, and I have always loved him. But I know that the great man distrusts and even perhaps fears him. The truth is that each must play his part even though they are in conflict, even though they will never be brought into harmony this side of the grave.

'I shall never see you again, but it is enough that we have seen each other and loved each other with a love that cannot be destroyed by time because it is not subject to time. Remember me. In my heart there will always be written the name —'

Peroni gazed dumbfounded at the page, for it seemed to him that his own name was written there. Then he realised that the name could not be Achille but Aquila, but as he looked more closely at the leaping, impetuous handwriting Aquila was transformed into Achille.

He moved to pick up the page, but in the instant he touched it, it crumbled into a negligible scattering of the finest yellow dust.

If you have enjoyed this book and would like to receive details of other Walker Adventure titles, please write to:

Adventure Editor
Walker and Company
720 Fifth Avenue
New York, NY 10019